SAY YES

DARA GIRARD

ISBN: 978-1949764352

SAY YES

Published by ILORI Press Books

ILORI PRESS BOOKS, LLC

P.O. Box 10332

Silver Spring, MD 20914

www.iloripressbooks.com

Table for Two

Gaining Interest

Careless Rapture

Dangerous Curves

Familiar Stranger

It Happened One Wedding

Unexpected Pleasure

Midnight Promise

Sweet Temptation

Always and Forever

Truly Yours

Clifton Sisters

The Sapphire Pendant

The Amber Stone

The Emerald Ring

Fortune Brothers

A Tempting Proposal

A Seductive Arrangement

Novels

Honest Betrayal

The Daughters of Winston Barnett

Remember My Name

Illusive Flame

Winterwood Lane

Promise Me

DEAR READER LETTER

Dear Reader,

Welcome to the sixth book in the *It Happened One Wedding* series where the best part of the story comes after "I do."

Catching the bouquet.

I've seen my share and it can either be a fun joyous tradition or a humiliating debacle.

For Nicole Harrison it ends up being the latter. And worse.

Much worse.

But this story wouldn't be a romance if it ended there. So enter Jayden Cassell her reluctant rescuer.

He's the one man who will force this marriage-shy woman to start hearing wedding bells of her own.

I enjoyed the twisty, surprising romance of Nicole and Jayden and hope you enjoy their story too.

All the best,

Dara

You can find out more about this series and learn about my other titles on my website www.daragirard.com

CHAPTER ONE

The guests were already placing bets.

There were few in the wedding party on the bride's side who thought Ernestina Jayne Brown Harrison Dell Young's fifth trip down the aisle would last longer than a year. But no one would argue that the fifty-eight year old bride looked stunning in a peach colored chiffon gown with cap sleeves and keyhole back.

Ernestina's beauty had been the talk of the Jamaican parish where she'd been the daughter of a school head-master and a postmistress and that talk was no different in the Georgia town where she'd settled for the past twenty years.

The bride's remarkably smooth brown skin, that made her look two decades younger, noble features and expertly dyed black hair, which she kept in twists that fell to her shoulders, did not go unnoticed by the maid of honor who did her best to school her features and make sure no one could guess what she was thinking.

Dressed in a cool blue mermaid gown, the woman could have upstaged the bride, not only because she was younger or because she was just as striking in terms of her beautiful features and brown skin, her natural black hair swept back and held together by clips, but because everyone wanted to know what Ernestina's eldest daughter thought of this most recent event.

Nicole wouldn't give them the pleasure. She was used to being on display—she'd become part of the second wedding party at five years old and had held that distinction ever since—and other people's whispers. Her mother's lifestyle always provided fodder for the small Jamaican immigrant community.

She knew people wanted to catch any telling expression on her face (at thirteen going on fourteen she'd made the mistake of crying in public when her mother made a match she hated and that had been part of the rumor mill for years) and she wouldn't give them the satisfaction.

Over the years she'd learned to guard herself and protect her mother, even though her mother didn't feel she needed to. Ernestina seemed impervious to what others thought of her. But Nicole cared and she would see this day as a success no matter how hard enduring it was for her.

She would pretend to be happy for her mother and the tall, silver haired man who stood with a beaming smile by her side. Nicole sighed annoyed with herself. It was probably time to remember the poor man's name. She'd have to pay attention to what the pastor called him. She'd gotten in the habit of dismissing the name of any new man in her mother's life since they usually didn't last long. She could almost gauge their longevity by the latest app update on her phone to know how long they'd be around. But this one...Damn what was his name? It had been on the invitation... He should stick out in her mind since he had managed to convince her mother to marry him.

Although that wasn't a grand feat. Getting Ernestina to take a walk down the aisle didn't take much persuasion. Compliment her (You're so beautiful and sweet), her two daughters (You've raised them so well), her home (I've never seen a woman with such fine domestic tastes) and Ernestina was a lost woman. It didn't hurt if the man was financially viable and had a healthy sexual appetite—not that Nicole wanted to know how vigorous. Although her mother liked to remind her that she was "still a woman" not that Nicole ever doubted that.

She only wished her mother wouldn't act like a woman of twenty-three. Her mother wasn't as sweet as she appeared and graded most of her men as bananas and plantains depending on their length, fullness and her desired satisfaction (Too much information, Mom, Nicole had frequently reminded her without effect). Dating was a game to her and marriage the ultimate prize.

Nicole hated feeling so cynical. She'd done a background check on him—Prentice Clive, that's what the pastor called him—as much as she could find and he passed the test. A widower who'd been married thirty years before his wife's passing. He'd worked at the same insurance company in the days when that was even possible, for the same thirty years and had three grown children. He was stable and sensible.

At least Nicole hoped so, although she wondered how sensible a man could be marrying a woman with four previous husbands.

Ernestina's first husband had been a youthful, impulsive choice. She was a good girl of seventeen who wanted sex so she married her boyfriend. That marriage had lasted two years.

Then she'd met Nicole's father through a family friend. That union had lasted long enough to instigate a move to the US, produce two girls (they didn't get married until Ernestina was expecting Stephanie), and a gambling habit. His not hers. And Norman Harrison liked to gamble on whether a married women's husband would find out about him or not.

After seven years he lost that gamble and ended up getting shot by one of his lover's husband. He'd managed to live—the angry husband hit in him the fleshy part of his backside as he escaped out the window-and now resided peacefully with his third wife in Ohio. Nicole had a half-brother from that pairing.

Her mother's third husband was a charming rascal who Nicole never trusted, but who could make both her mother and younger sister squeal with delight from surprise trips to the store, returning with flowers and sweets. Also, within two months of marriage, he managed to surprise them by developing a mysterious back pain that made it impossible for him to work. Her mother supported all of them by becoming a top-rated realtor. That marriage lasted long enough for Nicole to catch him having a private session with a chiropractor. She'd been old enough to realize that a man with a bad back shouldn't have been so agile, with a woman's legs wrapped around him.

Her mother's fourth husband had been a nice change. Nicole had been starting her first year of high school when her mother married Neil. She'd liked Neil. Neil had been funny.

Neil had been dashing.

Neil had been a thief.

He nearly bankrupted her mother before she decided to divorce him. It was then that Nicole realized what her career goal would be. Psychology. She studied to become a marriage counselor. Since she'd been the one her mother had turned to after every broken marriage, she thought she had a natural gift that others would pay for. She could listen well and liked to make sense of things.

But while she enjoyed helping others—she had a very busy and successful practice which she ran with three other therapists—Nicole's own love life seemed to mirror her mother's. She never used the plantain and banana approach, although her mother tried her best to tell her about her detailed rating system, but she still ended up choosing duds. Fortunately, she'd had the sense not to get married.

Unfortunately, she liked the same type of men as her mother: Good looking, smart and successful. Was that so wrong? Was it wrong to have standards? But that hadn't worked out at all.

Her sister, Stephanie, seemed to have gone the complete opposite route of their mother's and had found gold. The computer science teacher had met a quiet guy at an AI conference. She found a man who wasn't particularly handsome (although he had kind eyes) nor successful (he'd been working on his PhD in theoretical computation while working at a retail store) but they fell in love and had been happily married for nearly six years and had a little girl. Nicole loved her brother-in-law but likened him to finding a four leaf clover. Very rare.

She'd seen the behind-the-scenes discord of too many couples to know that that kind of marital bliss was rare.

And now her mother had thought she had finally met The One. The love of her life. The man with whom she wanted to spend the rest of her life.

"Are you sure?" Nicole had asked her mother six months ago when her mother flashed her engagement ring while she and her sister sat across from her in Applebee's. Her mother's hand motion had happened so often before, Nicole had a brief sense of déjà vu. She went through all her ages—five, eight, thirteen.

"Of course I'm sure," Ernestina said with a tiny pout. "He's The One."

Nicole pushed aside her tomato basil soup and rested her arms on the table. "This time you're doing a pre-nup and—"

Ernestina kissed her teeth in disgust. "You're so unromantic."

Nicole couldn't understand how her mother still could be searching for romance after so much heartache. Her mother didn't wear rose colored glasses. She lived in a rose colored bubble. "After Neil you should be too."

Ernestina twirled a strand of hair around her finger and smiled like a lovesick teenager. "He's nothing like Neil. He has his own money and he's so good looking."

"Mom," Nicole said with a sigh. "Please, listen to me. A pre-nup won't take long and if he really loves you—"

"If you loved me, you wouldn't ask me to do something so horrible and trust me."

"A pre-nup isn't horrible. But if you don't like the idea then consider pre-marriage counseling—"

"Why would I need counseling for that? I know how to be married."

"But Mom—"

"And I've been without a man for so long. Almost fifteen years."

Nicole fought not to roll her eyes. "You haven't been without a man longer than a week. You've had five boyfriends since Neil. Six if you count—"

Ernestina made a dismissive wave of her hand. "Who's counting?"

"I am. And I'm saying that—"

"All those other men were just for fun. Marriage is different and I've learned from all my previous ones. I'm older now—"

"It would be nice if you acted like it," Nicole muttered getting a swift kick under the table from her sister.

"—and I know this time will be different," her mother finished.

"We're happy for you," Stephanie said. She reached across her grilled chicken salad and took her mother's hand to inspect the ring further before she sent Nicole a look through her dark rimmed glasses. "Aren't we?"

Nicole plastered on a smile. "Right. Thrilled. Delighted. Absolutely—" She stopped and winced when her sister pinched her and sent her another warning look not to overdo it.

Tears came to Ernestina's eyes. "You don't know how much that means to me. He really wants you to like him."

Nicole frowned. "We're not living with him so it doesn't really matter—"

"Of course we like him," Stephanie said, adjusting her glasses. That was a warning. Anytime her sister adjusted her glasses she was agitated about something and right now Nicole knew what. While Nicole had spent most of her childhood being her mother's confidant and taking care of whatever mess the various men left behind, Stephanie made it her habit to be the cheerleader. No matter how bad something was she would see the bright side. And seeing her mother happy was always her biggest priority.

Nicole got the hint and brightened her voice. "Yes, he's very clean."

When Ernestina lowered her gaze to dab tears from her eyes with a napkin, Stephanie nudged Nicole with her arm, narrowed her eyes and mouthed "clean?" to which Nicole shrugged in response. It was the best she could come up with. Her mother had dated this man for only three months, and Nicole had only met him two times and that was only because she'd made an effort. Her mother liked to keep her boyfriends to herself.

"We'll have a wedding in the spring," Ernestina said. "I'll need your help."

"Not again." Nicole winced but didn't stop when her sister kicked her. "Couldn't you do the Justice of the Peace this time and have a small gathering later?"

"This event is something we both want to share with family and friends. I already have an idea of the dress I'll wear."

"This is—"

Stephanie abruptly stood and adjusted her glasses again. "Mom, will you excuse us?" she said before she left the table and headed to the ladies' room.

Nicole knew she was in trouble. The glasses adjustment was one thing, but her sister always had a walk and tone when she was angry. She sighed and followed her.

"What is wrong with you?" Stephanie said the moment they were alone.

Nicole tapped her chest, shocked. "Me? Am I the only one hearing all that she's saying?"

"She wants to get married—"

Nicole's brows shot up. "Is that a surprise?"

"That's not the point."

"What is the point?"

"I just told you," Stephanie said, slowing her words as if Nicole was having difficulty understanding them. "She wants to get married."

Nicole feigned a look of amazement. "Really? Is this the first time?"

"She wants to get married again," Stephanie repeated in a firm voice.

"Again."

"And she has the right too. She has waited over a decade."

Nicole nodded and scratched her nose, pensive. "You know there are actually women who don't remarry at all. It's amazing how they find other things to do."

"You know that's not Mom and you shouldn't make her feel bad for wanting companionship."

"I don't have anything against her having companions —and you and I both know she's never without them—it's getting married again that makes me nervous."

"Marriages can work."

"I know that."

Stephanie folded her arms, her face growing solemn. "I'm not sure you do. You only see marriages in crisis."

"I also have clients who no longer need to see me anymore. I'm not against marriage in general, just Mom's in particular. I mean the men she chooses are—"

"It's not for us to judge. You did a background check and he's clean, right?"

Nicole nodded.

"So support her."

Nicole rested her hands on her hips. "And it doesn't bother you that Mom's paying for the entire wedding?"

"It's her special day and she has the money."

"I'm sure he knows that."

"He's paying for the honeymoon."

"Motel 6?" Nicole muttered under her breath not sure Ernestina's new man would splurge on something grand. "Ow!" Nicole said when her sister punched her. She rubbed her arm and said in a hurt tone, "What was that for?"

"Even if this is a giant mistake we have to be there for her. That's the only way to keep her safe. The moment we disappear from her life the vultures will settle in. Now let's go. We can't keep her waiting."

Her sister had a point. Which was why Nicole was

at the wedding, in the wedding party—again, ugh!—holding a bouquet she wanted to flatten between her palms and throw at the large cathedral window. She wore a dress that had gotten a whistle from a man and a wink from a woman. Her mother had deliberately chosen a slim-fitted gown. "It's about time that man you're seeing pops the question," Ernestina had told her, "and if he doesn't, perhaps you'll catch the eye of someone else who will."

Her mother was aggravating like that. She didn't care if her daughter outshone her if that meant the possibility of another wedding on the horizon.

That morning Nicole half thought of pretending she had the flu so she could escape the entire event.

But then she met her sister inside the church as guests were beginning to arrive and that option disappeared. Her sister looked gorgeous and green. "What's wrong?"

Stephanie took an ominous swallow. "I think I might be pregnant again."

"You know how babies get made, right? The USB goes into the portal and—"

"Shut up." Stephanie covered her mouth and groaned. "Oh God, I don't think I can make it."

Nicole pulled out a ginger chew from her handbag and handed it to her. "This might help. I'll tell Mom—"

Stephanie started to chew quickly. "She's depending on us. Nothing can go wrong." She took a deep breath. "I can do this—" She paused, covered her mouth and ran to the toilet.

So Nicole ended up alone. She ended up enduring all

the whispers and looks on a day she wished she could have avoided.

But that wasn't what she dreaded the most. She knew it wouldn't be just her mother who would notice she was dateless, but her relatives. Namely her Aunt Cleo. Her mother's younger sister who prided herself on having twice her sister's looks and thrice her sense.

Nicole half hoped her aunt would get lost at Heathrow Airport (taken by gypsies, never to be seen or heard from again, was also an appealing option) and not be able to make it. But she had made it. All five foot ten inches of her dressed in a black and red dress as if she'd stopped off at an expensive boutique before arriving there. Her aunt also schooled her features, giving no hint to what she was thinking. People would only see an attractive woman with a short hair cut and long dangling earrings with her dark gaze fixed front.

But once the ceremony ended and the new bride and groom kissed, Nicole inadvertently caught her aunt's gaze and in one awful moment they were in agreement—they knew they were witnessing another possible disaster.

CHAPTER TWO

"This one is more ridiculous than the last," Aunt Cleo said, her island lilt clipped by studied English disdain as she looked at Prentice talking to one of his groomsmen.

Nicole cast her eye around the hotel's outdoor courtyard where the reception was being held. Wrought iron tables and chairs sat expertly displayed along the paved stone terrace framed with cypress trees and an assortment of blossoming azaleas. Her mother had chosen to get married in late March just for that reason. She loved azaleas and hadn't been disappointed. "Careful, Aunty," Nicole said taking two champagne glasses from a passing waiter and handing one to her aunt, "someone might hear you."

Her aunt tended to pretend to speak in low tones, but was always loud enough to have her voice carry. Nicole was never sure if her aunt was hard of hearing or just being cruel.

She took the glass from Nicole. "How did your sister manage to get out of this fiasco?"

"She wasn't feeling well."

"Beat you to that excuse, did she?" Aunt Cleo said with a knowing grin.

"She wasn't lying. She really looked ill."

Aunt Cleo looked at the groom again then at her sister who stood chatting with one of her friends. "I don't know why your mother had to get herself another husband."

Nicole took a sip of her drink and said in a low voice, "As opposed to someone else's?"

Her aunt pursed her lips and didn't respond. Cleo had been the well-kept mistress to a diplomat, ambassador and top MP before settling down with a man who either didn't know better or had the confidence not to care about her history.

After a long enough silence to make Nicole feel uncomfortable she said, "How long has it been since the last one?"

Nicole didn't misunderstand her. She knew her aunt was referring to her mother's weddings and not her men. "Long enough."

"Is there a reason you're being vague?"

Yes, so that you'll change the subject. "Over a decade."

Her brows shot up. "My how time flies. I suppose I can't blame her then. Who was the last one? Nigel?"

"Neil."

"Her mid-life crisis I suppose," Aunt Cleo said with a shrug. "But a woman should never be so desperate."

"She truly loved him at the time."

Her aunt sent her a long look. "I noticed you didn't come with a date."

Nicole inwardly groaned. She knew it wasn't something that could be avoided, but it was also something she didn't want to discuss. She'd hoped that people would pay so much attention to her mother that no one would notice that her boyfriend of three years hadn't shown up.

She'd known there was a possibility of trouble in her relationship with the handsome podiatrist when Richard had taken her to her favorite restaurant. It was a fine dining place situated inside a Greek revival-styled mansion that offered a traditional buffet-style southern cooking experience. The location had put her on alert. She'd dubbed the restaurant their "make up place" because he always took her there to apologize.

Like when he cheated on her (It was just once, baby, she didn't mean anything to me), when he'd skipped out on an event with her to have game night with his buddies (Baby, I didn't realize how much it meant to you) and then when he took money from Nina—her wallet (I was going to pay you back).

So when he surprised her with a trip to the restaurant and led her to sit in the green and burgundy dining room, with its crystal chandeliers and antique tables and chairs, Nicole searched her mind, but couldn't figure out what he'd done wrong, so she suspected the worse. But then he started complimenting her. He never did that. Ever.

He started telling her how impressed he was with her successful business and how beautiful she looked in her dress. That's when her heart fell. She'd been down that road before. She held up her hand half-way through her chicken and dumplings.

"Break up with me afterwards," she told him.

He stared at her open mouthed, after telling her what a great body she had. "What?"

"I just need you to show your face at my mother's wedding then we'll never see each other again."

He sat back. "Who said I'm breaking up with you?"

"Aren't you?"

He hesitated. "Well...sort of but—"

"But what?"

"You make it sound so cold."

"I'm making it exactly what it is. A parting of ways."

He pointed at her and frowned. "See? That's what's wrong with you."

Nicole's brows shot up. "Me? You're blaming this on me?"

"You don't care."

"Of course I do. Do you really think I enjoy a guy taking me to my favorite restaurant just so that he can tell me I'm a great lay but I'm not for him?"

His frown deepened. "I didn't put it like that."

"Five minutes."

"What?"

"That's how long you spent talking about my body."

"It's a compliment." His eyes scanned over her form with appreciation. "You've got a great one."

"And that's all you noticed."

"I mentioned you being successful too."

"One minute."

"What?"

"That's how long you took telling me about my success."

He threw his head back, stunned. "You're actually timing me?"

"I was timing myself to see how long it would take me to figure out what you'd done wrong. Then I realized it was me. I was the problem."

He sighed. "Listen, baby, I'm sorry."

"I know."

He sent her a long look. "I never got the sense you cared about me."

"I do care."

He shook his head. "You never act like it. Even now it doesn't feel like anything has changed."

She'd never give him the satisfaction of knowing how much he hurt her. How much this moment made her want to scream and ask him why all she'd given him hadn't been enough. All the apologies she'd accepted, all the disappointments, all the loneliness. Lonely. All the men she'd been with had made her feel that way. But she wouldn't let him know that. She wouldn't let him know that she'd buy herself a bottle of red wine and cry until her throat was sore and her body ached. She didn't want him to leave her. She wanted a man who would stay. A man who wanted to be with her. A man who could love her. But she wouldn't tell him that either. She knew that men lived on that kind of weakness in a woman. Instead she stabbed a dumpling with her fork and said in a cool voice, "If I burst into tears would you stay?" And she held her breath half hoping he would say yes.

He sighed with regret. "I'm traveling for business the day of your mother's wedding. I'm sorry."

If only I could believe you were really sorry. "I know."

He'd at least formerly dumped her and had paid for a fine meal. Her ex before him had been less kind. He'd just tossed her green plastic toothbrush in the trash bin and replaced it with another one (a hot pink mechanical brush with different tips, she still wondered if there was a hidden meaning there) and before him there had been a guy from college who had thrown a tantrum, throwing dishes and crying, when she'd gotten into her chosen grad school and he hadn't. He said he never wanted to see her again.

She'd had hopes for Richard. She'd been understanding and patient. And now she had nothing to show for her three years. She'd spent the past two months pretending to be in a relationship that wasn't real anymore just to avoid questions. But no one could avoid her Aunt Cleo. "He couldn't make it," Nicole said, hoping to sound nonchalant instead of bitter.

Her aunt's keen gaze studied her. "Is he ill too?"

"No."

"I see."

I truly hope you don't.

"There are better men out there."

Nicole finished her drink.

"And what you need is someone in-between."

"In-between what? Puberty and adulthood?"

"No, this is completely different. When you've come out of a long-term relationship you're still vulnerable. You need something absolutely diverting and inconsequential. If you let me, I can select someone suitable."

"Thank you, but no," Nicole said, pretending her aunt's words hadn't intrigued her. She did like the idea. An in-between guy. Hmm...

She was tired of the men she'd chosen. Tired of being hurt. And she was hurt. She'd been hurt by her father and her stepfathers and her boyfriends. She was not going to jump blindly into another relationship, but she didn't want to be alone either. She needed a distraction. A rebound relationship sounded perfect. Fun even. Something that didn't mean anything, that would eventually end but would prepare her for the next relationship.

But no. That wouldn't work either. Finding another man wasn't the problem, her track record was. She didn't want to be like her mother going from one relationship to another. She needed a change. A drastic change. And this was the moment to start. Nicole felt suddenly renewed.

The white, red, pink, and purple azaleas suddenly looked brighter, the sky bluer. She had no reason to be upset. A wedding was as good a place as any to find a new guy. However, most of the other guests were older than she was since they were made up of the new couple's friends. But if she met someone older, she was open to that too.

Her aunt began to grin. "I believe I've caught your interest."

"I'm pondering the idea, but not in the way you think," Nicole said as she let her gaze skim over the crowd. She lost hope of finding anyone interesting then she saw a bear standing alone at the bar.

CHAPTER THREE

He wasn't really a bear, of course. Bears didn't come to wedding receptions dressed in tuxedos. But the man definitely reminded her of one for some reason. He was big and brown with black hair and a beard.

He wasn't her type at all, taller and heavier than she liked her men and not particularly handsome in the conventional sense, but at least he looked around her age, early to mid thirties, and there was something about him that intrigued her. It could have been the way he leaned against the bar like a man used to being alone and liking it. The other guests kept their distance.

"Don't even smell it," Aunt Cleo warned her in a curt tone.

Nicole turned to her aunt surprised. It wasn't like her aunt to be so definite when it came to a man. "Why not?"

"He came with his mum."

Nicole looked at the bear-man with surprise and a

little disappointment. He didn't look like the type. "Really?"

"Yes." Aunt Cleo nodded to a little woman in a cherry red hat and pink dress talking to her mother. "That one."

"That tiny thing is his mother?" Nicole said amazed. She remembered briefly meeting the button nosed woman with round cheeks when she'd saved the woman's hat from being stepped on when it had blown off her head.

"Yes."

"My goodness his father must be enormous." Nicole glanced around to see if there was anyone resembling him, but couldn't see anyone.

"His father's passed." Aunt Cleo shook her head, stopping any questions. "I briefly spoke to her, but that doesn't change anything. Move on."

"Just because a man comes with his mother—"

"Move on."

Nicole cast another look at him. She didn't mean to stare but there was something about him that looked so out of place. Like an elephant surrounded by ducks. He seemed to dwarf everything around him. He carried himself well, but there was an air of mystery about him.

He suddenly lifted his gaze and their eyes met.

No, they collided. She felt as if the space between them had melted away and she stood only a foot away. Nothing else existed but him. This big, magnificent man. His gaze caught and held hers for a moment before he looked away. Seconds had passed but it felt like a lifetime. Her heart raced, her skin tingled. No man had ever had that effect on her. Why would he? Why wasn't he talking to anyone? Why was he alone?

"He's incredibly close with her," Aunt Cleo continued. "I think he might even live with her."

Nicole inwardly groaned. That information instantly took him off the list. Even she wasn't that desperate. She sighed disappointed, she'd have to look elsewhere.

Aunt Cleo delicately cleared her throat. "However, if you'll let me—"

"I'm fine, Aunty," Nicole said in a firm voice. "Thank you."

"I'll be around for two weeks in case you change your mind."

I won't. "Thank you."

Aunt Cleo fell silent before she cleared her throat again. "Have your standards changed? Or are you still closed minded?"

"Still closed. I don't date married men."

"They make life interesting without any of the hassle."

"No."

She shrugged. "Your mother gave you the wrong rules of life."

"How would you like to know that your significant other is stepping out on you?" Nicole asked referring to her aunt's husband who hadn't been able to make it to the wedding.

"He isn't."

"But if he were."

"He isn't. I know how to choose my men. Unlike your mother." Aunt Cleo glanced at the man at the bar then met Nicole's gaze and said with a condescending smile, "Unlike you."

Nicole opened her mouth to respond but before she could her aunt rolled her eyes and said, "Oh dear, you'd better get ready."

"For what?"

"Your mother's about to toss the bouquet."

"So what?"

"At least pretend to catch it. Your mum will try to throw it at you."

"I told her not to."

Her aunt shoved her forward into the crowd of women. "When will you learn that your mother rarely listens to you?"

Nicole stumbled forward and caught her mother's searching gaze. She shook her head. Her mother only smiled in response and turned then threw the bouquet over her shoulder directly at Nicole.

Nicole could have caught the bouquet if she'd wanted to, which she didn't, however, she didn't get the chance to even try since someone elbowed her in the eye, knocking her backwards. She collapsed and hit her head on the paved ground while above her, the woman who had knocked her down, grabbed the bouquet only to have it quickly snatched by another woman, who also lost her grip on it, casting it through the air again for someone else to seize.

In their pursuit, two other women bumped into each other and fell on top of Nicole. Within seconds catching the bouquet became a frenzy. Nicole turned on her stomach and struggled to crawl her way out of the pile.

She heard her dress rip and smelled the warm brick pavement, imaging the dirt staining her dress red; her nails scrapped across it as she tried to get out of the madness, but she felt herself being crushed. People were so engrossed by the sight of women fighting for the flowers that no one noticed her on the ground. She looked up (her right eye throbbed, swelling shut and her other eye was blurry) between taffeta, silk and stockings to a freedom that seemed yards away.

Great. Just great. Was this how it would end? Trampled to death? She made one last valiant effort to free herself, reaching her hand out as far as she could reach and to her relief and surprise she felt a large, warm hand wrap itself around her wrist and in one forward motion she felt herself being pulled free.

CHAPTER FOUR

For one crazy moment she felt as if she were flying through the air before she collided with something both hard and soft that smelled like whiskey and peppermint. She blinked her good eye and saw white buttons and a man's chest.

Nicole squinted up at him, but the late afternoon sun cast his face in shadow so she lifted her chin a little further then stumbled back as the world began to spin.

"Are you okay?" he asked in a sharp voice. His voice was deep like rocks at the bottom of the ocean.

"I'm fine," she said automatically even though she didn't feel that way. "I just need to sit down." She felt that same strong hand on her arm and let it guide her, limping, since she'd lost a shoe, to a seat. "Thanks for helping me."

"Hmm," he said, the sound coming out like a low growl, as he pressed something soft against the back of her head. Which she thought was strange since it was her eye that was killing her. But the pressure felt good.

"I can't believe I got hit by a woman reaching for the bouquet."

He didn't sit down and when he spoke his voice seemed very far above her. She thought she heard the hint of an island accent but wasn't sure. "I think you should see a doctor. Are you feeling dizzy?"

She stared at his waist not daring to lift her head as she'd tried to before. "I was a little at first, but it's stopping now. Really, I'm just embarrassed."

"There's nothing to be embarrassed about."

"Who gets a concussion grabbing a bouquet?"

His tone sharpened. "You think you have a concussion?"

"No, I was trying to be funny."

"Concussions aren't funny. I didn't realize catching a bouquet was a blood sport."

"In my family it is. But from now on I'm staying courtside."

"Seems safer."

"Could you sit down so that I can see your face?"

"Why?" he asked and his voice softened and became more distant as if he'd turned his face away from her. "There's nothing to see. You really need—"

"You don't have a face?"

A note of humor entered his voice when he spoke. "No."

She tugged on his trouser leg. "Then this I definitely have to see."

"First let me get you—"

"Please."

The man sighed then took the seat in front of her without removing his hand from behind her head, making the gesture strangely intimate. With just a slight move she could rest her cheek against his arm.

"Better?" he said.

She blinked her good eye a few times, but it continued to water so his features and shape remained a blurry mix of brown and black. But from his build, rather than his face, she could tell he was the tall, husky bear-man she'd noticed at the bar. "No, I can still hardly see you. You don't have to keep pressing the back of my head. It's my eye that feels like it wants to pop out."

"I'm not surprised," he said in a low voice, but he didn't remove his hand. He looked around. "Who did you come here with?"

"I drove myself."

He softly swore then took one of her hands and pressed it against the cloth on the back of her head. Why was there cloth there? "Hold still," he told her. "I just need to tell my mother that you need more than a glass of water and then I'll take you to the hospital."

"I don't need to go to the hosp—"

But he moved too fast. Faster than she would have thought for a man his size. He was overreacting. But at least she was away from everyone for a moment. Nicole took the cloth from her head then stared down at it stunned. It was a lovely, multicolored scarf, the white edges bright against the large red stain in the middle. Blood? She didn't remember hitting her head that hard. The sky and grass seemed to spin once more.

She collapsed against something both hard and soft again.

"I've got you," a familiar male voice said. "I told you to keep the pressure on." He didn't sound angry but something about his tone let her know something had upset him as he took the scarf and pressed it on the back of her head again before he placed her hand over it. He sat down in front of her then slid her lost shoe back on her foot. "Keep holding it."

"I don't understand," Nicole said suddenly uncertain of anything.

She was usually more sure of things, but right now nothing made sense. The lightheadedness, the blood on the scarf, the pain in her eye, this stranger. She blinked again and her eye was less blurry than before allowing him to come into focus. He wasn't bad looking and had dark eyes—the eyes of a protector. That surprised her.

"Think you can stand?" he said.

"Um...yes?"

She let him help her to her feet and they started walking to the parking lot.

"My scarf!" a woman said behind them. "You're stealing my scarf!"

Nicole felt the man stiffen, but his voice remained soft. He turned around. "No, just borrowing it. As you can see she's been hurt and needs—"

Nicole vaguely made out a woman in a green dress that stretched to the floor. "What I need is my scarf back. I got it on my trip to Spain!"

"I'm sorry, but this is an emergency. I'll—"

"I don't care." The woman held out her hand and

Nicole saw a fat wrist with thin bangles. "I want my scarf back."

"I'm afraid that's not possible."

"Of course it's possible. It's right there."

"She needs it. Excuse me." He turned.

"You're *refusing* to give it back to me?" the woman called after them. "This is an outrage!"

"What is going on here?" a commanding voice said.

A voice that made Nicole groan. Her Aunt Cleo could make a simple misunderstanding turn into a melodrama.

"This couple is stealing my scarf," the woman said.

The bear-man didn't deny the charge, but said, "I'm taking her to the hospital," before he continued to lead Nicole away.

Aunt Cleo blocked him. "I'm sure that's not necessary."

His tone hardened. "I don't have time to argue with you right now. My car is right out front and—"

"I don't know who you are."

"I can vouch for him," another woman said. "He's my son."

"That doesn't—"

The man motioned to something in the distance. "That woman got her glasses smashed, another may have a busted nose and a third is barely walking straight. I think there are other people and things you could pay attention to." He sighed. "Mum, do you mind staying here and putting things right? I'll be right back once she's been seen."

His mother nodded.

He looked at the other woman. "And give this lady the twenty-five dollars she really paid for this knockoff scarf she's accusing us of stealing. Now if you'll excuse me."

Aunt Cleo cleared her throat. "I don't think—"

Nicole felt rather than heard the man take a deep breath before he addressed her aunt. "Unless you have the ability to sanitize and stitch this gash on the back of her head, with all due respect, I don't particularly care what you think." He nodded to his mother. "She's your assurance that I'm not a killer. I will come back for her."

Aunt Cleo made a small gasp but didn't respond.

Nicole had never heard someone be so forceful with her aunt, making her speechless. She wished she'd been in a better shape to enjoy it.

She didn't remember much after that. A car ride surrounded by the scent of lemon and lime; voices—one deep (his) replying to the cool and efficient questions of the ER doctor (hers); a white pillow and striped curtains; the feel of something tugging on the back of her head, a large hand holding hers; wanting to speak but feeling too tired to; drifting off to sleep then waking up to the sight of a red stain on something white; drifting off again; a nightmare she couldn't remember; a soothing deep voice; waking up feeling less tired and in less pain. Her vision was no longer blurry and she turned her head on the pillow and saw the bear-man sitting by her bed.

She looked at his shirt and saw an arch of red across his white shirt. Blood.

"Oh no. I'm so—" She stopped when he held up his hand.

"Stop doing that."

"What?"

"Apologizing."

She bit her lip. "How long has it been?"

He didn't answer right way instead his dark brown eyes studied her. His gaze was too intense, which unnerved her. She wasn't used to a man she didn't know paying such close attention. "Feeling better?"

"I feel like digging a hole and crawling inside."

"Why would you want to do that?"

"Embarrassment."

"There's nothing to be embarrassed about."

"How long have we been here?"

He turned away and watched a nurse hurry past. "You'll be ready to leave soon."

Which meant he wasn't going to tell her.

When they returned to his car, the sun had disappeared from the sky replaced by a black night peppered with stars. "It's been hours, hasn't it?" Nicole said as he started the car.

"Put your seatbelt on."

She did feel happy to feel more alert and her eye didn't throb, but she didn't like him avoiding her question. On the drive back he didn't talk much and the silence made her feel awkward. She looked at his shirt.

"I'll pay for the dry cleaning."

"No need. It was an accident."

"How about lunch, then?" she asked as he stopped at a red traffic light. "My treat."

He turned to her and flashed a smile so warm and full of humor that her mouth suddenly went dry. He was better looking than she'd first thought. The unexpected expression softened his features so much that he looked attractive in a way she hadn't noticed before. "Ask me that when you're not under the influence of heavy medication."

She frowned. Her mind felt clear, why would he think it was a joke. "I won't change my mind."

The light turned green and he turned away. "I doubt you'll remember asking me," he said in a low voice as if to himself.

"What's your name?"

"Jayden."

"Do you have a last name?"

He sighed. "Since you're not concussed it should be safe for you to close your eyes a bit."

"But I'm not tired."

"Just a couple minutes. We'll soon be back at the hotel and I'm sure your family will have a lot of questions."

Nicole put her head back and closed her eyes, knowing he was right. She'd have to have all her strength to face Aunt Cleo again. She only meant to rest her eyes and didn't remember falling asleep.

CHAPTER FIVE

His body felt like it was on fire.

Jayden Cassell prided himself on keeping his distance. He was careful not to touch anyone. He hadn't in years both by design and sheer will. He'd even stopped hugging his mother.

But then his mother, of all people, had forced him to break his rule.

"She's going to get crushed," his mother had said after the bouquet toss had turned into a rugby match. Jayden instantly saw who his mother was referring to. He saw the woman on the ground and raced towards her. He didn't think about what it would cost him.

He went into action and grabbed her.

He should have just dragged her out. Pulled her to safety. That's all she needed. But instead he'd briefly pulled her to him, instinctively, as a way to protect her, and the moment her body had collided with his had felt like a bomb, shattering the carefully constructed walls he'd built around himself.

His entire body hurt as if it were on fire. Like he'd come in from the cold and his limbs were thawing. It burned, seared. His throat closed, his tongue felt heavy in his mouth.

And he'd felt everything. The soft natural curls of her hair brushing against his chin, the curve of her arm, the sound of her dress brushing against his jacket, the scent of her (a strange mix of vanilla and peaches). If he hadn't seen the thin line of blood streaming down her neck, he would have pushed her away and pretended nothing had happened. Then he would have gone into the men's room and washed his neck, face and hands until they were red raw and he could feel numb again.

But she was hurt and she needed help. She needed him and she'd awakened something inside him. A desire. A dangerous, intense, lingering, insistent desire.

With effort he pushed it down and grabbed the first thing he could find to control the bleeding. He remembered his mouth feeling dry, his palms sweaty as he took the scarf that was draped over the back of one of the chairs in the courtyard and placed it against her head.

Five times.

He'd had to touch her five times and each time hurt more than the last. Twice before arriving at the hospital and three times there. But he had no choice. She needed help. It didn't matter that his skin was screaming as if a series of nails were being dragged down his skin. He gritted his teeth when she took his hand as she lay in the hospital bed. Her brows were furrowed and he couldn't tell if she was in pain or having a nightmare. Her hand seemed to sweep along the edge of the bed as if she were groping for something. He offered his hand, half expecting her to ignore it, instead she held on tight and the furrow between her brows eased. He knew it was an unconscious gesture but he felt a building anger.

But he didn't know where to focus it. He couldn't be angry at her. He was the one determined to take her to the hospital. If he'd left her at the wedding reception this wouldn't have happened. But he was still angry. Angry that she was able to casually touch him no matter what looks he gave her. Twice he'd shot her a warning glare as a warning, but either she was too confused to notice or didn't care or he'd lost his touch.

That glare had been honed through necessity and had kept him safe. To see a woman totally oblivious to it was defeating. But five was enough. He'd reached his limit.

But then she kept apologizing. How could he be angry at someone who also made him feel guilty?

But then she did give him a reason to be angry. She shouldn't tease him. Lunch? Really?

Jayden glanced at her as she slept. She must be as high as a coconut tree if a woman like her would even think to look at a guy like him. Not that there was anything wrong with him. He'd been told he wasn't bad looking and he cleaned up well, but she was in a different league entirely. He knew the kind of guy she was usually with—sparkling teeth, lots of money. He'd been tempted to say yes. He was tempted to say *hell yes*. She was beautiful and she was kind. From a distance he'd watched when she'd saved his mother's hat from being stepped on when it had blown off her head.

"This is a beautiful hat," she'd said, making his mother smile. His mother rarely did lately. That alone had softened his heart towards her, but then she did something else. She paused and turned the hat over and studied it before she said, "Did you design this yourself?"

"I know it looks cheap."

"Oh no," she said quickly, "that's not it at all. It's the hand stitched detail that caught my eye. This is one of a kind. You've got a gift." She lifted the hat to replace it back on his mother's head. "Do you mind?"

"No, please."

"And this time we need to pin it properly so it stays in place." She secured the hat then nodded, pleased. "Perfect."

"Thank you," his mother said then let her gaze follow the woman the rest of the day, which was why she'd noticed her in the crowd before the bouquet was tossed. His mother stood beside him and clasped her hands with joy. "Oh good. Look at that. She's still single."

Jayden sniffed. "You say that as if it's supposed to mean something to me."

He was in no mood to meet anyone. He was stuck in a place he didn't want to be, wearing a suit that was too tight. But he hadn't been in a suit for a while and certainly not since his life fell apart and his breakup. A breakup so bad he'd gained twenty pounds and lost any interest in women for the foreseeable future. All that mattered now was taking care of his mother and keeping her safe.

Growing up, his mother had been both his hero and the source of his greatest embarrassment. Although she raised two sons she kept boxes of feminine hygiene products that she made available to the nurses' station at three high schools, a local homeless shelter and community center. Many times she was so focused on her mission she would forget about other things. His childhood was filled with memories of her forgetfulness.

Twice he'd found a handful of tampons packed in his school lunch instead of carrots sticks.

It was not unsurprising to see sanitary pads tucked between car seat cushions so he always cringed anytime she offered to drive his friends home. As a child and teenager he didn't understand why she felt so compelled to help girls who couldn't afford basic needs until she finally told him the story of a friend who had missed many days of school because she couldn't afford them. She loved helping others. So when she needed his help he didn't hesitate to do what he needed to. He wouldn't have had it any other way.

But he'd never take being safe for granted again.

At least they weren't in Tennessee anymore. Thankfully, that hellish past was behind them.

Jayden tugged on his penguin suit glancing at the bride before she threw the bouquet, she had such joy on her face one would have thought it was her first wedding, but if the rumors were true it wasn't—far from it. However, his mother had begged him to come with her so that she wouldn't be alone. But he knew the real reason she asked was because she was worried about him being alone.

He didn't want to give her anything more to worry about. Her dear friend was getting married and she wanted to attend. They'd met at their popular bi-monthly book club. Although whenever he asked his mother about the books they discussed she usually had a hard time remembering the titles. It seemed to be a gathering more for drinking and eating than reading and discussing books.

But she was happy and safe.

That would all change if he didn't do something soon.

Presently, she walked with a cane after breaking her hip eight months ago and stayed in a rehabilitation facility. Her accident had aged her considerably. Looking at her now she wasn't the fighter she used to be. He would fight her battle for her. But her latest battle worried him the most. In two weeks she'd need to be re-housed. The rehabilitation center wasn't a permanent arrangement and a long-term care facility was out of his budget so he didn't know where to put her. She couldn't stay with him, but finding somewhere else had been harder than expected.

He never let on that finding her a permanent place was a problem. He took her to the wedding and didn't care if she worried about his single status. It was better than her worrying about where she was going to live next. He'd figure it out. He always did.

But that meant he had to remain focused. He hadn't been in Georgia long enough to let down his guard. Doubt he ever could. He couldn't afford friends, not yet anyway, and women were a distraction he didn't need.

Especially women like this. A woman who could turn a church aisle into a fashion runway, a woman who could make his mother smile, and make him feel things he had no business feeling. No, she was off-limits. He knew she wasn't really in her right mind. At the hospital she kept calling him "Brown Bear" making everyone smile and making his face burn. She said it with such affection it sounded like a nickname between lovers. Something they definitely weren't.

Jayden caught sight of the hotel, where the reception was, standing tall, its lights bright against the night sky and felt some tension ease. He parked the car, eager to part ways, turned to her and said, "We're here."

She didn't move.

He raised his voice. "We're here." Still nothing. His heart picked up speed in alarm. He put his ear to her mouth and felt her warm breath. She was alive. His heart rate returned to normal.

She was still breathing. Good. He flexed his hand and softly swore. Too bad she was a heavy sleeper. He'd have to shake her awake. Unfortunately, that would involve touching her again and he didn't want to do that.

He thought for a moment, drumming his fingers on his knees, then came to a solution. He backed out of his parking spot, sped around the lot then drove back into the empty space coming to a hard stop, jerking her forward, the seatbelt keeping her from flying too far forward. "Sorry about that," he said as she sat up, rubbing her eyes. "Didn't want to miss my chance to get the space."

She stretched her arms out in front of her. "We're already back at the hotel?"

"Hmm."

She unlatched the seatbelt and opened the door. "Thanks again."

"You're welcome, Nicole."

She beamed. "You know my name?"

After nearly four hours I'd better. "You said your name at the hospital."

"Oh right. What was your name again?"

"Doesn't matter. You'd forget it anyway." He headed towards the hotel lobby. He'd called his mother to let her know he was returning and learned that the reception was over, but that he was to meet her in the lobby. He paused when he realized Nicole wasn't behind him. He turned back to his black Lexus and saw her looking over the passenger seat. "Did you lose something?" he asked her.

"Checking to make sure I didn't get blood on anything."

"It's okay."

"I'd feel awful if I did. I already ruined your shirt and—"

"I'll deal with it. Come on." To his relief she stepped to the side and let him close the door. Then she did something awful.

She wrapped her hand around his arm and said, "Coffee then."

He swallowed hard, wondering how best to move away. "What?"

"Would you prefer to go out for coffee instead of lunch?"

Right now he couldn't think about coffee or lunch

or even breathing until he could get away from her. Until he could remove himself from the feel of her fingers around his arm. The pressure seeping through the protection of his jacket and shirt. But she didn't really know what she was doing or saying so he couldn't get upset with her. He had to be patient and understanding. The best way to do both would be to lie. "Sure."

She smiled with such joy he felt a little guilty. "Really?"

"Hmm."

"Do you know that place off of Harrow Street?"

He nodded.

"Say ten on Saturday?"

She wouldn't remember this conversation let alone him. If he could make her happy for a few more minutes, what was the harm in that? He led her through the glass hotel doors and walked into the lobby, measuring every step. Each step got him closer to freedom. "Sure."

"I look forward to it..." She let her words fall away, waiting for him to tell her his name again.

"Jayden Cassell."

He didn't know why he'd given her his full name, but felt he owed her.

"Wow. You're only the second Cassell I've ever met. Do you have a sister by any chance? I work with a Cassell."

"Nope."

She didn't have a chance to ask him any more questions because the woman from before (the fashionably dressed one not the owner of the cheap scarf) and the bride came and whisked her away, peppering her with questions.

Jayden released a sigh. He hadn't realized how tense he'd been until he saw her leave. Ever since she'd bumped into him he'd been on edge.

And seeing her hurt reminded him too much of...

No. He wouldn't think about that. This time it had been an accident and he'd been able to help. He'd done something right. He hadn't come too late.

He gripped his hand into a fist as he watched his mother coming towards him, concern on her face, her hand on her cane. He never wanted to be too late again.

CHAPTER SIX

"You did what?"

Nicole shifted her gaze from her aunt to her mother. The two women had bullied her into the honeymoon suite of the hotel and forced her to lie on the bed. "I really don't need to lie down, Mom."

Her mother rubbed her hands together, her voice anxious. "Are you sure you're okay?"

"They wouldn't have released me if they hadn't been sure."

"Clearly you need your head reexamined," her aunt said. "You asked him out?"

Nicole sat up and rested against the plush headboard. "I'm treating him to coffee. It's the least I can do for all his help."

"I told you he's not a prospect. He's—"

"A banana or plantain?" her mother asked.

Nicole waved her hand dismissing the idea. "I just met him and I've told you I hate that rating system."

She shrugged. "You can come up with your own, but—"

"That's beside the point," Aunt Cleo said. "You have to change your mind and—" She paused and looked at her sister who was sniffing and wiping her eyes. "What's the matter?"

"Is this a bad sign?" Ernestina said.

"What?"

"One daughter gets ill and another gets hurt on my wedding day. Perhaps—"

Aunt Cleo kissed her teeth in irritation. "Don't be stupid."

Her mother's lower lip trembled. "It was supposed to be a perfect day."

"And it was," Nicole said, wishing her sister was there instead of her. She knew what to say to make their mother feel better. "You looked beautiful and the guy is happy. You said he is The One. In a few hours you'll be together on your honeymoon."

"But—"

"Stop searching for misery," Aunt Cleo said. She glanced at the door. "Your new husband will be wondering what's wrong."

"Where is Pendelton?" Nicole asked.

"Who?" her mother asked.

"She means Prentice," Aunt Cleo said. She sent Nicole a stern look that silently said "You should know that. Maybe your head injury is worse than you think." Nicole looked away.

Her mother sniffed. "He's in the lobby."

"Tell him everything's fine," Aunt Cleo said. "I'll take care of Nicole and we'll be gone before you return."

Nicole blew her mother a kiss. "See you when you get back from Barbados."

Ernestina nodded then left. Once the door closed Nicole turned to her aunt and said, "It's just coffee."

"Coffee can always turn into lunch. And lunch can lead to...many different things."

That was what she was hoping, but she wouldn't tell her aunt that. But he had caught her interest. He didn't seem the kind of man tied to his mother's apron strings. Perhaps he was just being a good son and doing his mother a favor. She planned to find out more.

Aunt Cleo sat on the side of the bed and pointed at her. "Take that look off your face."

Nicole blinked quickly. "What look?"

"The look your mother gets any time she passes a jewelry store with a ring in the window. The look that says 'I want one of those.'"

"I'm not interested in marriage."

"No, you've never been interested in marriage for yourself, but that doesn't mean you can't get into trouble."

"It's just coffee."

Her aunt narrowed her eyes. "Why him?"

"He helped me."

"You were keen even before that."

"Because he's different. He's unlike any other guy I've gone out with before."

Aunt Cleo snapped her fingers and nodded.

"Exactly, which is why it will be a disaster. Why won't you let me—"

"Because we don't have the same taste in men."

"Which is why you keep getting men who don't work out. It's not too late to cancel."

"Why would I want to cancel?"

"Because he's not your normal type—"

"Which is a plus."

"And he's hiding something."

Nicole paused, surprised. "How can you know that? You just met the man."

Aunt Cleo tapped the side of her nose. "I have a gift for these things. He's not in-between material."

"It's called rebound and if I wanted, and I'm not saying I do, to have him, then it wouldn't matter what he was hiding because I don't plan to make it last long. Don't worry. It's just coffee."

Her aunt stood, smoothing down her dress before she sent Nicole a look of warning. "Make sure it stays that way."

CHAPTER SEVEN

"She was pretty," Dionne Cassell told her son as he drove her home. Traffic was congested as people made use of what nightlife their small Georgia city had to offer on a Saturday.

"I didn't notice," Jayden said. "The black eye and blood must have gotten in the way."

"Don't be facety."

He sniffed, amused. "Have you forgotten who I am?"

"I'm so glad you were there. She could have gotten seriously injured. Nobody was going to help. They were too busy holding their phones up and recording that terrible scene."

"It certainly was memorable."

"She's Ernestina's daughter."

"Hmm." His mother had already told him that twice. First, when she'd caught him staring at Nicole as she walked down the aisle (as if she should be wearing a crown) and again at the reception before the bouquet toss. Try as he might he couldn't not look at her. Not because she was attractive, that was a given, but because she kept looking at him.

It put him on edge. He'd done his best to try to appear as invisible as possible, which wasn't easy at his height and size, but he'd managed pretty well, which was why he was alone at the bar, watching everyone else.

Staying away, being an observer, had kept him safe. It was a hard earned skill.

But Ernestina's daughter wasn't following the rules.

She was supposed to ignore him, look through him, see past him. Not look at him and catch his eye and smile with invitation. It was an invitation he planned to refuse. Even if she hadn't been Ernestina's daughter he would have stayed away, but it didn't help because if she were anything like her mother, she had a number of men in her past or was looking to get married and he didn't want to fall into either category.

"Thanks for coming," his mother said. It had been the tenth time she'd told him that. She always repeated herself when she was nervous.

He sighed. "What's on your mind?"

"I know how much you didn't want to go."

He shook his head. "That's not what's bothering you."

"She was pretty."

He couldn't stop a smile. "You already said that."

"I'm waiting for you to admit it too."

"She actually asked me out."

His mother's face brightened. "That's wonderful."

"She'd also suffered a head injury and was on drugs at the time."

"I'm sure she meant it."

"Sure, now tell me what's really troubling you."

His mother opened her mouth then closed it defeated when he shot her a look. He wasn't in the mood for lies. "Why can't I live with you?" she finally said.

He gritted his teeth. He should have known that was coming. "I told you my place is too small."

"I won't take up much room. I hate the thought of you trying to find somewhere else for me. I could take care of things for you."

"You need space to heal."

"I'm much better now. It won't be for long. Please, Jayden let me—"

"It's out of the question. I will find you a place. Don't worry."

"How come you make me feel like a burden?"

He sighed. "You're not a burden."

"Then why won't you—"

His tone hardened. "Because I can't, okay? It's not happening so change the subject."

She fell silent and stared out the window. He kept his gaze ahead, sorry that he'd lost his temper, but it couldn't be helped.

He'd tried to connect with his brother, Brian, but he refused to help.

His conversation with him only a couple days ago had gone worse than he'd hoped.

"I just need you to take her for a couple of months, that's all," Jayden had told him over the phone while on break at his job, the sound of moving equipment loud in the background.

"You know I can't do that," Brian said. "Why can't she get a place?"

"She can't work—"

"You mean she won't."

"She's too young for Social Security and she can't stand long because of her hip so getting a job or working is out of the question and—"

"She can find a job where she can sit down."

"She's not an office worker. Never has been."

Brian sighed annoyed. "You're still protecting her."

"She's our mother."

"Does she even know what that means?"

"Watch it."

"Admit it. She's a burden."

Jayden counted to ten. Getting angry at his brother wouldn't fix anything. His mother's situation hadn't always been this bad. Before this she'd lived with her mother the past five years in a tiny, but comfortable house outside of Atlanta. But then when Gran died, the proceeds from the sale of the house, split among her and her three siblings and had only given her enough money to last a year. Then she'd gotten injured. After taking a shower she'd slipped—having not installed the bathmat he'd told her to use—and broken her hip. The cost of the surgery, medicines and doctor appointments quickly ate up most of the money she'd received.

He wasn't in the position to care for her. The rehabilitation center had been perfect. But getting her another place in a good neighborhood had proven a challenge.

Her credit was bad and he couldn't use himself as a reference, without repercussions. It wasn't how he'd imagined his or her life turning out but he had no regrets. She was safe. He'd protect her, continue to protect, her no matter what.

"What am I supposed to do?" he finally said.

"Besides get on with your life? Haven't you sacrificed enough for her?"

"I'm not asking you to agree with my decision. I've never asked you for a favor like this before. But—"

"I'm not going to let her ruin my life the way she did yours. One of us needs to escape from this."

"It wasn't her fault."

"It was all her fault. She had so many chances. You didn't need to rescue her if she'd rescued herself first. Look at all that you've lost. She's living her life. She's going out and you're still in prison. No matter where you go. It changed you. It changed me. She's the one who's remained unchanged."

"You know that's not true."

His brother's voice filled with emotion. "Do you know why I can't see you? Why I stay away? Because I hate what she did to you. I hate it every day. You were my hero. I looked up to you. You had everything and she made you—"

"She didn't make me do anything," Jayden said in a tight voice. "The choice was mine."

"Always protecting her. How come she never protects you?"

"I don't need anyone to protect me."

"Really? Remember when you were nine years old?"

"Don't go back there."

"Why not? While she was playing the saint to everyone else because she liked the attention, she left you at that doctor's office for three hours. Dad had to get off work."

"It was one time."

"You were the one who looked after me."

"You were too young to remember all that she—"

"No, you keep telling me things that didn't happen. She wasn't really there for us."

"She was in her own way. A little absent-minded but she loved us."

Brian paused. "How much do you need?"

"I don't need your money just let her stay—"

"I can't take her in. How much do you need?"

"Forget it." He disconnected. He knew it was pride. He should have taken whatever money his brother had to offer, but he didn't want to. Sometimes money wasn't enough.

But as he looked at his mother's profile briefly lit by the streetlights lining the road, he wondered if he'd made the right choice. He had lots of secrets.

He had secrets that he had to keep and never let her know. One was that in three hours, twelve minutes and thirty-four seconds he'd be sleeping in his car.

CHAPTER EIGHT

They should have never gotten married.

Ben Horowitz should have taken one look at Amelia Bethal and run for the hills. Better yet, taken a jet rocket because there was no way he could have managed to escape her grasp when she'd hooked eyes on the tax attorney and his sizable trust fund. Not that she was a gold-digger. That was too simple a term for a woman who'd survived being abandoned by her mother at the age of thirteen and dealt with a melancholy father who had the habit of giving her a good slap every now and then to show her how much he loved her. Apparently he loved her a lot. So Amelia ran away and learned that money was a great equalizer and set out to get a guy who would provide that.

Unfortunately, she should have also chosen someone who actually liked to spend money. But Ben was the kind of guy who would hold onto a penny until it squeaked. And he had his reasons. His father's bankruptcy had never left him and although the family eventually recovered to their former glory the recovery had been hard won.

The problem wasn't with either Ben or Amelia. They were both fine people on their own and with other more understanding spouses they could find happiness. But together they were like fire and gasoline. And Nicole was finding it difficult to help them see the other's viewpoint. They were too busy wrapped up in their own pain to see the pain they were causing each other and their three children.

But she was being paid to help them. Although Nicole thought she'd have better luck turning lightning into silver. She wasn't so fatalistic with most couples. With most she could find a glimmer of commonality. But with the Horowitz, even mention of the kids didn't stop the insults from flying. They barely tried any of the exercises she'd given them. She half wondered if she should recommend them to someone else. Maybe she'd become too jaded to see hope anymore.

That had been a fear of hers. Less and less she'd seen any hope of true reconciliation between the couples who came to her and she wondered if it was coloring her therapy. Perhaps she'd lost her fire.

"Well, we'll address that next time," she told Ben when the therapy session ended. The couple sat on opposite sides of the grey couch. The blue wallpaper around the room was supposed to be calming, like a sea breeze but, for some reason, today the color made Nicole think of drowning. "But for now I really need you two to try the exercise I gave you last week. It's important to break patterns and replace them with new ones."

"Like a marriage?" Ben said.

"What's that supposed to mean?" Amelia shot back. "You don't want to be married to me anymore?"

"If I had wanted a divorce I wouldn't be coming to therapy."

"You're probably too cheap to get a divorce."

"Do you even know how much these sessions cost?"

Get a divorce already! Nicole wanted to say. There was a level of disdain that had colored any previous feelings they'd once had for each other and without respect, there was little to work with. But she'd learned to be professional. It wasn't her place to tell them what to do, if they wanted to save a sinking ship that was also on fire that was fine by her.

Nicole slowly rose to her feet and said in a soothing tone, "What have we learned about escalating?"

They both turned to her and sighed. "It leads to pain," they said in unison.

"So what's the best way to deescalate something?"

"Not assume that the other person is insulting you," they again said in unison.

"Yes, a misunderstanding can quickly turn into something worse when accusations are thrown. Now let's try this again. What did you hear Ben say?"

"That our marriage is a bad pattern," Amelia said.

Nicole nodded and turned to Ben. "And what did you actually say or rather mean?"

"That there are bad patterns in our marriage."

"Good." Nicole opened the door. "That's a good start

to seeing how you can argue about something that was never said."

"If he'd said it that way, I wouldn't have misunderstood him," Amelia mumbled as she walked out the door.

"If you weren't always jumping down my throat maybe you'd hear me for a change," Ben muttered behind her.

Nicole closed the door and sighed. She had twenty minutes before her next appointment and needed the break.

It had been three days since her mother's wedding and she'd had to use a lot of makeup to cover up her bruised eye and had to style her hair in a creative way to cover over the bald patch where she'd gotten stitches. Fortunately, none of the witches noticed.

That's how she affectionately thought of the three other therapists she worked with at Our Love Counseling. Carla Cassell specialized in newlyweds. Yasmine Holmes focused on premarital and then there was Kelvin Nguyen who ran the group therapy sessions and was the most dangerous of all.

He pretended to like her but she knew that he wanted her office. It was dubbed "the Queen Suite" because of the size and view. He was jealous of her clients (she had a high referral rate) and her larger percentage of the business proceeds. If he moved her out there would be a three-way split instead of four. He had a smile as genuine as a toothpaste ad and a walk that commanded attention. But he wasn't as shallow as he appeared. He was smart, successful, and good looking and if they hadn't been colleagues and she hadn't put him one level above pond scum, she would have gone after him.

She'd dubbed them the witches because they always seemed to be huddled together talking behind her back. She didn't care. She liked what she did and as long as the business was solvent and she had a schedule she could control she was fine.

"You did something with your hair," Kelvin said when Nicole left her office to take a brief walk outside before her next clients arrived.

"Trying something new."

He tilted his head to the side and studied her. "And make up."

She glanced at his wrist. "And you got a new watch." It wasn't really a watch. It was a flashy silver object that likely cost the equivalent of someone's mortgage payment for two months.

He smiled, self-satisfied. "Just a little treat to myself."

She smiled back knowing his favorite subject was himself. "I know you deserve it. I'm just going for a quick walk." She moved past him feeling his gaze on her backside. He thought he was discreet, but she always knew he was looking. It was something else she put up with it.

Once outside in the landscaped medical center courtyard Nicole took a deep breath of the cool air, feeling on edge. She knew it wasn't Kelvin's fault. She was happy. Her mother and Prentice had arrived safely in Barbados. She'd already sent Nicole pictures of their adventures. Her mother genuinely looked happy and Nicole hoped that happiness would last at least a few years before any cracks in the foundation started to show. If they ever did. Perhaps her mother had found The One finally. She only wished she could believe it. But it wasn't her mother that had her on edge. It was Saturday. She was actually a little nervous.

No, that was the wrong word, she thought as she turned a corner. Not nervous. Excited. She really looked forward to seeing him again in spite of Aunt Cleo's warnings. It was only coffee. She didn't expect much else, however, if one thing lead to another...

Her cell phone rang.

"It was a stomach bug," Stephanie said the moment Nicole answered.

"And you're happy about that?"

"I was out of commission for nearly three days and could hardly—"

"Don't need the details," Nicole said.

"But I'm so happy I'm not pregnant."

"Congratulations. Just remember that if the little USB goes into the port—"

"Shut up," Stephanie said without anger.

"Firewalls were developed for a reason."

"And that's about the depth of your computer knowledge."

"Exactly, but if you want an essay on the psychological effects of procreation I can enlighten you."

"I'd prefer you tell me about the wedding."

Nicole paused. "You haven't spoken to Aunt Cleo?"

"I've hardly spoken to anyone. I told you I—"

"Right," Nicole said quickly, sorry she'd brought the topic up again. "Stomach bug. So you—"

"I was practically hugging the toilet for days. This nasty bug had me beat. There was one time when—"

"Stephanie, I love you, but I don't want to know."

"Fair enough. Now tell me about Mom's wedding. Why would Aunt Cleo talk to me?"

If she hadn't mentioned Aunt Cleo she could have lied and said everything went perfectly, but their aunt only liked to spread juicy news so that wouldn't work.

"Mom's safe on her honeymoon," Nicole said, hoping to stall her sister long enough until she ran out of time and had to return to her office. "She sent pictures."

"What happened?"

Nicole sighed. She could just imagine her sister adjusting her eye frames.

"I'll tell you later. I have to get back to—"

"Fine, I'll talk to Aunt Cleo first and you can fill in any gaps later."

Nicole swore. Her sister was smart and knew that Nicole would not want her speaking to Aunt Cleo first. "I ended up at the hospital."

"The hospital?" Stephanie said shocked. "Are you okay?"

"I'm fine."

"What happened?"

She told her about the bouquet toss and skimmed over the events afterwards, editing some details.

"It's not like you to be so clumsy," her sister said.

"It wasn't me. Those women were vicious. You should have seen them. I don't think I was the only one who got hurt. I'm lucky I got out alive. It's your fault."

"How is it my fault?"

"If you had been there, I wouldn't have been manipulated by Mom and Aunt Cleo to be forced to participate in that humiliating, archaic ritual in the first place."

"How was the hospital visit? Meet any cute doctors?"

"I'm with Richard, remember?"

Her sister sighed. "The wedding's over, you don't have to pretend you're seeing him anymore."

Nicole paused surprised. "You knew?"

"The fact that you weren't complaining about him let me know something was up."

"I wasn't always complaining," Nicole said offended.

"One day he's forgotten this or done that and then for two months he's taking you here and giving you that. I knew something was up. But that's not important. Answer my question."

"You're not even curious why we broke up?"

"I'm hoping it's because you finally came to your senses."

"He dumped me."

"Only because you let him," Stephanie said without sympathy. "Now about the hospital—"

"He wanted me to act more hurt, can you believe that? Of course I'm hurt, but I'm not going to burst into tears in the middle of a restaurant. *Our* restaurant. And why did he have to break up with me there? It was my favorite place and now every time I go there I'm going to think of him talking about my thighs."

"What?"

"He said I had a great body and kept going on about it. I know it was a compliment, but it was annoying."

"Forget about him. You can take someone else there and make new memories. Now doctors—"

"He wasn't a doctor. He was a—"

"I'm not talking about him," Stephanie cut in with impatience. "I'm talking about when you went to the hospital. Did you meet any?"

"Plenty." She lowered her voice as if sharing a secret. "Did you know that hospitals tend to be filled with them? Isn't that amazing?"

"If I didn't love you..."

Nicole laughed. "The doctor who attended to me was very efficient and caring."

"And good looking?"

"Yes. *She* was very cute."

"Fine. What about nurses then?"

"Yes, the nurse was wonderful."

"A guy right?"

"Yes, he was nearing seventy and adorable."

"You are mean."

Nicole laughed again. "Aunt Cleo wants to set me up."

"Let her. It might be fun."

"No, she likes married men."

"She's changed."

"I can improve my love life on my own. Besides, I think I might have met someone."

"Who?"

"The guy who drove me to the hospital."

"I thought you drove yourself."

"I might have left out a few details."

Stephanie's tone grew excited. "Fill me in."

"This time you can ask Aunt Cleo to do that. She doesn't approve of him."

"Oooo," Stephanie said impressed. "This sounds good. Tell me more."

"I've got to go. But I'll call you Sunday."

After Saturday coffee with a guy with dark eyes and teasing grin, Nicole hoped that by Sunday she'd have a lot to share.

But after fifteen minutes waiting in the crowded coffee shop among the hiss of an espresso machine and the scent of sweet raisin muffins, Nicole knew he wasn't coming. Hope, however, kept her waiting for another twenty minutes.

Disbelief turned it into nearly an hour. She couldn't believe he'd stood her up. That wearing her favorite skirt, the blue one with the scalloped hem, and splurging on a limited edition deep hue lipstick, had all been a waste. She couldn't believe that Aunt Cleo had been right and he wasn't worth the hassle.

Twice she'd had to rebuff the advances of men who saw her alone and thought she didn't want to be. One was polite and cordial; the other took her disinterest as a personal rebuff and called her a few choice names before leaving.

Nicole looked at the coffee cup shaped clock on the wall over the counter and sighed defeated. She gathered her things (she'd even foolishly bought three muffins she thought he might like to try—one vegan and one gluten just in case) and returned to her car.

She stopped when she saw her grey BMW and the long

keyed mark of destruction that marred the entire side of it. She took a deep breath and slowly turned to see the second guy she'd rebuffed leaning against his car and smirking at her. He'd been watching her longer than she'd thought and knew what kind of car she drove. It should have frightened her, but instead she was angry. Angry at Richard for dumping her at her favorite restaurant, angry at a guy for standing her up without even a message to say he wanted to cancel, and then this jerk who couldn't take "I'm not interested" like a man. Nicole opened her passenger side door then tossed her handbag inside before she took off her high heels, slipped on her sneakers, turned and ran at him.

Full force.

His smirk quickly faded.

As she got closer she saw his surprise turn to fear then anger. He lifted his hands to defend himself, but he wasn't her target. She darted to the side and kicked the side mirror of his gold Honda, smashing it. It dangled like a deflated balloon. He stared at it stunned.

"Now we're even," Nicole said.

"You crazy bitch."

She bounced on her toes as if preparing for another round. "Yes, that's right. I'm crazy." She kicked his side mirror again. "You should have stayed away, because I was being nice the first time, but now I'm mad and I'm crazy." She kicked the mirror a third time. "Want to call the police? If you want to take me on that's fine. I'll go even crazier on you. I'll make you wish you hadn't looked in my direction, that you'd never even said a word to me. Is that what you want?"

He called her a choice foul name before he jumped in his car and sped away.

She turned and smiled for the CCTV camera that covered the parking lot then returned to her car and sat inside.

She gripped her steering wheel and swallowed hard. She was crazy. Completely crazy because she felt like crying and there was no reason to cry. Tears burned her eyes and that was stupid because there was no reason to feel so hurt. It was stupid to let a man hurt her again.

He was a stranger, she shouldn't have looked forward to seeing him again so much. She shouldn't have practiced the questions she was going to ask him or have taken so much time with her hair. It was all crazy, ridiculous. He'd lied to her. He wasn't who she'd thought he was.

Nicole straightened in her seat and took a deep breath, the threat of tears dissipating. She'd forget him. Just like she forgot all the rest.

Over the following two weeks Aunt Cleo returned to England, not before telling her "I told you so"; her mother returned from her honeymoon in high spirits; her sister returned to reminding Nicole that Richard was a jerk and Nicole's life returned to the way it had always been.

Until one rainy afternoon.

CHAPTER NINE

The Lowards loved each other deeply. They just didn't know it yet.

They didn't speak the same language of love. Every action the other did, that they in turn would want done for themselves, was seen as a sign that one didn't love the other. *She* thought the lemon cake he'd baked her for her birthday was an underhanded way to break her diet; *he* claimed he didn't know she was on a diet; *she* claimed he never listened to her. He was hurt that she missed his awards ceremony hosted by the local farmer's market for growing that largest cabbage that season. She claimed she'd told him she had nothing to wear to such a grand event and hadn't wanted to embarrass him.

But they were slowly making progress. Or at least that was what Nicole liked to tell herself.

A steady April rain tapped on the roof of the Sunrise Rehabilitation Center as Nicole ended her session with them. She came to the facility once a month to provide counseling for older couples, couples going through transitional phrases because of illness and disability, or those facing second marriages in later years (there were different adjustments to make at seventy-five than at thirty-five)and enjoyed the time she spent there. It was always nice to see individuals come to the facility barely able to walk or in wheelchairs, leaving using only a cane or with barely a limp and a new lease on life.

Nicole ended her session with the Lowards with words of encouragement before she headed to the front desk to say goodbye to the front staff. The sound of a low voice stopped her in her tracks. Her heart started to race. She knew that voice. That low deep grumble.

"I just need a little more time," he said.

"I'm sorry, Mr. Cassell," the registration attendant said with genuine regret, "but we can't extend for another week. We have a policy—"

"How about a couple more days? It doesn't need to be a full week."

"And we need that room for—"

"It doesn't have to be that specific room. My mother isn't particular and I don't care if it's smaller. Please. Just give me some more time to—"

"She has to be out in two days. I'm sorry." The attendant turned away from him and returned to her computer.

He didn't move from the counter, he continued to rest against it, but Nicole saw his large shoulders sag. He was having a bad day and she knew she was about to make it worse, but she didn't care. It was his fault she'd waited nearly an hour and gotten her car keyed.

She tapped him on the shoulder. "Excuse me."

He turned around, looking both tired and sad, which annoyed her because she wanted to be angry at him but couldn't. "Yes?" he said his tone uncertain, his gaze wary. He was a man on guard. She didn't blame him. He'd have to come up with a great lie for standing her up.

She waited for a sign of recognition, but he stared at her without a hint of any. Her patience snapped. Really? She was that unremarkable that he'd totally forgotten who she was? "I'm Nicole. We met at my mother's wedding. You drove me to the hospital."

He blinked surprised. "You remember me?"

She frowned. "Why wouldn't I remember you?"

The guarded look left his eyes replaced by the intense, protective gaze she'd remembered from before. She felt some of her anger subside, replaced with confusion. "How's your head?" he asked.

"It's fine. It's what happened afterwards that hurt more."

"Afterwards?" He straightened to his full height alarmed. "Something else happened?"

She nodded. "Yes, this guy stood me up."

He shoved his hands in his jeans pockets and bit his lip. "I really didn't think you'd remember."

She folded her arms. His words didn't make any sense. He was very memorable. "I waited an hour. Even bought you muffins."

He ran a hand down his face. "I'm sorry. I really didn't think you'd show up."

"I told you I would."

"I didn't believe you."

"Are you busy? Because if you're not there's a cafeteria and you owe me coffee."

Minutes later they sat in the sparsely populated room with two cups of coffee and for him a chicken sandwich, bag of cookies, chips, two apples and an orange.

"So I couldn't help overhearing you talking to the front desk," she said since he wasn't keen to say anything.

"It's nothing."

"I think I can help you. If you need a place for your mother I have an extra room." She held up her hand. "Think about your mother before your pride."

"Don't worry, I don't have much of that left." He hesitated. "How long can she stay?"

"How long do you need?"

"A couple of months."

She stroked her chin, thoughtful. "That's going to cost you."

He released a long sigh. "How much?"

"Three dates with me."

CHAPTER TEN

He was hallucinating.

Jayden blinked and finished his coffee in one long swallow. He was hallucinating because he hadn't eaten breakfast or lunch. It was worth the sacrifice and had allowed him to pay for his mother to stay another week in the facility. He planned to eat dinner later before he went to work at the warehouse.

Hunger.

That had to be why he felt lightheaded and saw a sexy angel sitting in front of him offering him salvation.

He slowly set the cup down, pleased his hand wasn't shaking. He'd imagined it. She wasn't offering to let his mother stay with her in exchange for three dates. That was impossible. He'd never been that lucky before. This was all a dream.

"Well?"

He lifted his gaze. She was still there, but he didn't dare touch her to make sure she was real. Even though he wanted to for a number of reasons. He gripped his hands into fists on his lap.

"You really have to think that hard?" she said.

He shook his head. "It's not that. I don't understand."

"What's not to understand? Three dates in exchange for your mother staying with me."

Jayden absently stroked his beard both amazed and curious. She was just as attractive as he remembered her. And he was glad to get to see her without a swollen eye and blood on her clothes. But he couldn't figure her out. She was not the kind of women who would have a hard time getting a date. Perhaps she was speaking in code. Maybe she wanted more. The exchange didn't seem equal. "Just three dates?" he asked, wanting to be clear.

"Yes, of course. What else..." Her words faded away, slow dawning entered her face as her gaze swept over his body, taking in every inch of him. For a moment he felt stripped bare and liked it. She then looked up at his face horrified. He turned away to keep from laughing. "No, I didn't mean...my offer came out wrong. I don't want sex... I mean I'm not against it..." She shook her head. "I only want to get to know you better."

He bit his lip. He rested his arms on the table and said in a low voice, "The answer is yes either way."

"Yes?"

He nodded. He was desperate. He didn't care what she thought of him. He was never supposed to see her again. Especially not like this. He only hoped she wouldn't change her mind.

"Okay." She drew out the word and looked down.

She looked flustered and unsure. Jayden sat back and

sighed with regret. He'd been too eager and had scared her. He shouldn't have hinted that she wanted him for his body. She was getting nervous. In a few seconds she'd come up with a reason to leave and then change her mind.

He pushed his chair back and started to stand. If he left, she wouldn't get scared and only think about his mother. She wasn't a threat. "I should go."

"Not yet," she said, covering his hand with a strong grip that surprised him. And feeling her touch hurt just as it had the first time like a shock of electricity. He pulled his hand away but she didn't seem to notice as she took out her cell phone. "Wait, you don't even know where I live and does your mother have any dietary restrictions? Do you need to hire a home aid? Can she do stairs? If she can't, I think I have another room that's better."

Jayden clasped his hands together to keep them from shaking. He was the one in trouble. She was just as kind as he remembered her to be. "Excuse me for a minute," he said, but he didn't give her a chance to respond before he left the cafeteria.

He went to the men's room and washed his face. Could he really pull this off? He had to pretend to be someone else for three dates. If she wanted to come to his place he'd lie. He'd gotten good at it. It was a risk, if she ever found out the truth about him his mother would be in trouble. But he just needed the time to place her somewhere else. He grabbed a paper towel and dried his face. He could do this. He had to. And it wouldn't be hard.

He returned to the cafeteria and didn't see her. He

walked up to their table and saw his sandwich and fruit. Had she tricked him?

"Are you ready to go?"

He spun around relieved. She hadn't left him. "Leave?"

"Yes, to talk to your mother."

"She can't know that—"

"That you offered your body?" Nicole said with a smile. She winked. "I thought that would be our little secret."

She might think it was a joke, but he was serious. His mother couldn't know that he'd struggled to find her somewhere else to stay. "It's not that. She doesn't...I'm working, I just—"

"I'll tell her that I needed the extra money and persuaded you to let me rent the room to you for her. Sound good?"

Perfect. "Thanks." He gave her his mother's room number then let her walk ahead of him. He released a sigh. For now his mother was safe and so were his secrets.

CHAPTER ELEVEN

Dionne wanted to be happy, but the guilt wouldn't leave her. It lingered. It squeezed life from her. All she could think about was what her son had sacrificed for her. He told her he was fine but she knew that was a lie. Jayden hadn't lied to her before. But he wasn't the man he used to be. She had no one to blame but herself.

She went to the large window in a room that would soon no longer be hers, and rested her cane against the windowsill, pleased the rain had stopped. He'd found a new place for her to live and yet a sense of relief didn't come.

She'd raised a good son. A good man. Although he'd not given anyone the chance to see that now. He protected himself, guarded his heart. It hadn't always been like that. He'd once had a beautiful apartment, a fiancée. Lots of friends. And then...

She sighed. He would be so angry if he knew how she felt. And how cruel was it if she lived her life with regret after all he'd done for her? But she wanted to see him come alive again. She looked from her second story window and watched Jayden walk to his beloved car (a gift he'd received from his uncle upon graduation), avoiding the puddles. She saw Ernestina's daughter hurrying by his side trying to keep up and moving her hands while she spoke to him.

Dionne couldn't help a smile because if Nicole expected an elaborate response she would be disappointed. Jayden wasn't one to talk much even before now. However, she hoped the young woman would give him a chance and show him that it was okay to trust again.

Trust.

She'd been lucky to have trustworthy people throughout most of her life.

She'd been the sheltered and adored fourth child. When she'd met her husband she'd become the sheltered and adored wife. They'd had their two sons in America with dreams of a new life, before returning to Jamaica when her husband's father had gotten sick and needed help running his car repair shop. He took care of everything and she let him. She didn't mind. She trusted him and she loved him. He left her sooner than they'd both expected. Only forty-seven. But they'd had twenty wonderful years. She didn't regret that. She also didn't regret returning to America with her sons and living in Tennessee with her brother and his wife. They had the space since their children had moved out.

But she was lonely. She'd loved being a wife so when she met Henry Lucas she'd been ready. She'd waited nearly nine years. She was in her fifties and her sons were grown—one in college the other embarking on his career and she was ready to settle down again.

He wasn't particularly good looking, but he was charming and intelligent. He made her smile.

Jayden hadn't been too happy to return from a business trip, (conference or forum or some such thing she could never get them straight; by the time he was twenty-five most of the things he did she didn't understand) and discover she'd gotten married.

"Get it annulled," he'd told her in no uncertain terms while Dionne cleaned the table in her brother's kitchen. It seemed the best place to meet them and share her news. She'd wanted to protect her new home and husband from their judgment.

"I'm not a child. We wanted something simple and quick."

"Why?"

"I don't have to explain myself to you."

Jayden nodded. "You're right. You don't. He does. Where is he?"

She grabbed his arm. "Leave it."

He glared at his younger brother, Brian, who sat quietly at the table. At twenty-two he looked much younger. "What do you think about this?"

Brian shrugged. "It's her life."

"That's not an answer. Have you met him?"

"A couple of times."

"What's he like?"

"He seems nice."

"Five months. You've known each other for five months."

"We felt like we've known each other forever."

But she hadn't known him at all. She couldn't remember how soon after the wedding when he told her he didn't like her choice of shampoo. He said it smelled cheap and bought her another brand. Then he didn't like the lipstick she wore. Then he hated her favorite skirt.

Soon she didn't know how to cook his calaloo just right. The songs she liked to listen to were subpar. She'd tried to please him. Having grown up adored it had been strange to be with someone who was so hard to please. Her first husband had been easy. Henry said she'd been spoiled.

But why he'd had to hit her still confused her. She'd never made someone so angry in her life before. She didn't understand why he'd get into such rages. And nothing she could do would calm him down. Of course he was always so sorry afterwards and seeing such a big man cry always made her feel bad for him. He didn't mean it. His life had been hard and if she didn't upset him their life would be perfect.

Bruises had been so easy to hide in the winter. But spring and summer were difficult. She used to love to wear her sleeveless dresses, but that became impossible. She was too ashamed to tell anyone. Even the police. She wasn't one of *those* women. She had her pride. She was a woman of the middle-class. She wasn't one of those lowly immigrant women who find themselves in bad situations due to poor planning. She was a success story. She had a reputation to maintain. And the reputation of her sons.

If they knew...

She made it her mission that they would never find

out. Three years she managed to keep it secret. But of course they did eventually find out and that had changed everything.

Her bad choice had caused her to lose one son—Brian still refused to talk to her—and had ruined Jayden's life. He'd forgiven her, told her there was nothing to forgive, but she couldn't forgive herself. She needed a second chance to make things right.

Dionne leaned on her cane and walked back to her bed.

Ernestina's daughter was her chance. She was the kind of woman who could help her son find joy again.

CHAPTER TWELVE

"A re you free tomorrow night?"

That's what Nicole had asked him as he walked to his car. How could he say no? The faster he got the dates over with the sooner he could stop lying to her. Unfortunately, as he sat in the elegant surroundings of the restaurant she'd chosen, he realized that tonight was going to cost him a week's pay and his sanity.

He didn't mean to look at the prices. He never used to. He never had to, but it had become a habit and the moment he sat down and looked at the menu he felt the blood leave his face. Of course the moment she told him the address and he drove up to the reconstructed mansion he knew that it would be an expensive night. He just never imagined it would be *this* expensive. Even the buffet option was a stretch.

But he had to see this date as a rent payment. His mother would be moving in tomorrow. Several months for his mother to relax and not worry about anything.

Fortunately, he had a credit card he used for emergencies and he'd wait for Nicole to place her order before he said anything. If he was stuck ordering only a cup of coffee and biscuits that would be fine.

"This is my favorite place," she said. She'd dressed up for the evening; he didn't want to notice but couldn't help himself. She wore a red silk blouse and dark skirt with silver earrings.

Fortunately, he had a suit he used for interviews he'd bought at a thrift store so he didn't look too out of place. "Hmm."

"So order what you want. My treat."

He looked at her surprised. "What?"

She laughed. "You didn't think I'd make you pay for this, did you?"

He hesitated. "Well...it's a date."

"A first date. That would be mean. I'm not one of those food and dash dates who only goes out with guys to get a free meal. Plus Nina's ready to work."

"Nina?"

"My wallet. Calling her Nina is a habit I learned from my father. He named his wallet Nina too and told me it helped him pay attention to his money by giving it respect."

Jayden nodded. He guessed that made some sense.

"I later learned it was also the name of one of his women. But that's beside the point. I brought you here to help me get rid of a ghost."

"A ghost?"

She nodded then motioned to a table near one of the large windows. "That's where he dumped me. My ex."

"I see."

"So I need to make new and better memories here so that I can get rid of him in my mind." She tapped the side of her head for emphasis.

"I see," Jayden said although he didn't. It didn't feel right that she'd pay for the date *plus* let his mother stay with her. Where was the exchange in that? Even though he needed the help it made him feel awkward. *Forget about your pride, just eat. You haven't eaten this well since the wedding.*

Nicole tapped on the top of his menu. "What's the problem?"

"Problem?"

"You're frowning at the menu. Is there nothing you like?"

"I don't feel right not paying."

"Don't worry. You'll pay later."

"I will?"

She winked. "Well, you did offer your body, didn't you?"

"Hmm." He returned his gaze to the menu. He didn't want to think about bodies. Especially when she looked so good and he was hungry for more than food.

"Relax, just having you here is enough. Tell me about yourself."

That's one thing he didn't want to do, but since he would only see her two more times it didn't matter. "Not much to say. I work in computer consulting. I have a brother." It wasn't a complete lie. At the rehabilitation center he'd helped two residents with their computer issues. Naturally there was no reason to tell her that he had a PO Box with a street address so he could get mail; that he worked four times a week in a wine and spirit warehouse and also had a side business buying faulty laptops, mobile phones and cameras and refurbishing them for money.

"What brought you to Georgia? I heard you and your mother used to live in Tennessee."

"A new life." At least that was true. "I had a bad breakup and uh business went down."

"You owned a business?"

"No, the business I worked for got bought and I lost my job." Now that was a complete lie. He began to ask her a question when he saw her face change and got a sense she wasn't paying attention to him anymore. Then he heard one of the four women at the table diagonal from them say in a loud whisper, "Are you sure that's her?"

"It looks like her," the second woman said, "Nicole Harrison."

"Oh my god yes," the first woman said, "and look who she's with. Where did she pick him up?"

"Is she really with that guy?" a third woman added. "Did you see his suit?"

"I guess she got desperate after Richard dumped her."

"Did you see who he's with now? I'd be depressed too if I were in her shoes."

"And then there's her mother," the fourth woman said with a smirk.

"I *know.* Didn't she just get married for what...the seventh time or something?"

Jayden abruptly pushed back his seat and said, "Let's go."

Nicole looked up at him startled. "What?"

"They're ruining my appetite."

"But—"

"We haven't ordered anything and we can come back another time." Not that he ever planned to. He walked past the table, stumbling against it. The motion knocked two glasses of red wine which spilled on two of the women. They all jumped up. "You big, clumsy oaf!" the first woman said.

"Sorry about that," Jayden said without a note of apology. "The tables are too close together. It was hard to get past. As you can see, I'm a big guy."

The woman opened her mouth to say something insulting but the look in Jayden's gaze stopped her. She spun away and the three other women followed.

Nicole covered her mouth to keep from laughing as she headed for the door. Once outside she said, "That was mean."

"I wasn't lying, the tables are too close. Now let me show you a great place to eat without people bothering you."

Nearly a half hour later they stood inside a small Jamaican diner among the scent of curry and onion salt. He stared at the board. "This is my treat. Order what you want."

Nicole ordered red beans and rice with vegetable roti. He ordered fried plantain and curry chicken before they settled in one of the booths.

Nicole looked around at the brightly colored walls. "I didn't know this place was here."

He wouldn't have either if he hadn't been looking for something with good sized portions within his budget. He'd also found a soul food diner, Chinese takeaway and Italian restaurant that offered the same. He'd remember them for the next time. Otherwise she'd really cost him. "Hmm."

"I'm sorry about—"

Jayden set his fork down and lost his temper. "What is with you being 'sorry' all de time?" he said, a taste of his island background touching his words. "Sorry dis, sorry dat. Sorry fi what? Four hitety titey women, one with a face so ugly she could crack a mirror, with nothing better to do than to bad mouth others? You sorry fi dat? Is dat your fault?"

"It's embarrassing."

"Are you related?"

"No."

"Then why should someone else's bad manners embarrass you?"

Nicole nodded. "You're right. It's silly."

"Yes."

She rested her chin on her hand and grinned at him. "So the Southern boy has island roots, huh?"

"That's no surprise. Our mothers are friends."

"But I was born here," Nicole clarified.

"So was I, but I was four when my parents went back to Jamaica and I spent more than ten years there."

Nicole nodded again. "Which is why you gave me a proper dress down."

Jayden scratched his cheek, feeling his face burn, he hadn't planned to do that either. He'd let down his guard. "You were getting on my nerves."

"I know. Sorry I—"

He took a deep breath and gripped his fork. "Say sorry one more time and I'll..."

"Box my ears?" she finished with a teasing grin, knowing he wouldn't.

"If I knew you better I would. Someone should have by now. You can't go around apologizing for breathing. You're a successful, beautiful, intelligent woman. Who made you feel that way?"

"Nobody. Only me." She took a plantain from his plate and took a bite. "See? I won't apologize for that."

"That's dangerous to take food from a man's plate."

She lifted her fork and let it hover over his plate. "Really dangerous?"

He nodded.

She slowly lowered her fork.

"You're lucky I'm being nice."

She stole another plantain. "Thank you."

"Brown bear."

Her brows shot up. "What?"

"Do you remember calling me that?"

She covered her mouth. "When did I say that?"

"At the hospital."

"I said that out loud?"

He gravely shook his head. "No, I read your mind. Of course you said it out loud. More than once."

"I'm sor—I couldn't help it. It was what I thought when I first saw you."

"You saw me as a bear?"

She pushed her red beans around on her plate. "I like bears."

"Bears can be deadly."

"And cuddly," she said then scooped up her red beans and rice and took a bite.

"Only teddy bears."

"Or ones that are well-trained."

"Even trained animals can be wild."

"I guess I like that aspect too. What animal would you compare me to?"

"I don't know."

"Take a guess."

Jayden thought for a moment then said, "A turtle."

"A turtle!"

"Yes, I like turtles. I used to own one. A cute little thing that was very shy with everyone else except me. It took me a while to get her to let me feed her by hand."

"So you see me as a woman with a hard shell?"

Jayden shook his head unable to put into words what he thought. Why would a beautiful woman keep apologizing and pretend things were fine when they weren't? A soft smile touched his lips. "No, I see you as a woman who's still hiding."

HE WAS WRONG OF COURSE, Nicole thought as she drove home. She wasn't hiding. She spoke her mind and did what she wanted to. She couldn't believe he'd compared her to a turtle. Perhaps he didn't like her comparing him to a bear.

She softly swore. She couldn't believe she'd said that out loud, but it didn't change her opinion. When she stole the plantain from his plate, he growled like one and he had beautiful brown eyes. Not that she'd ever been close enough to a bear to see that, but she'd seen pictures.

He was a lot more fun than she'd thought he would be. He still didn't talk much, but it was refreshing to be with a man who seemed to like listening to her. He didn't make her feel bad about what they'd overheard those other women saying about her.

She was used to the whispers but what really made her skin burn was the thought of Jayden overhearing them. But spilling the wine on the women had just been petty enough to improve her mood.

Two more dates to go. She hoped to convince him to try many more. He was shy but interested. She could tell by the way she'd catch him staring before looking away. He was the one who was hiding. To get him out of his shell date number two would have to be strategic and seductive.

CHAPTER THIRTEEN

He knew Nicole had money, but he never imagined she had *this* much money.

Jayden stared in awe at the elegant bungalow style estate with a main house and attached cottage on a large landscaped, wooded corner lot in one of the older neighborhoods surrounding the city.

"How much are you paying her for this place?" his mother asked as they walked through the cottage to the bedroom. "I think it's too grand."

He set her suitcase down and stared at the four poster bed then looked around to see that the scent of fresh roses came from a bouquet near the window. It wasn't an ordinary room—it was a suite at a bed and breakfast.

He gripped the wooden post tempering down his joy. He had to take this as a good sign. His mother deserved this. Now his mother was safe and if his recent conversation with Mr. Ballard from the rehabilitation center panned out, he could find her a place just like it.

He hadn't expected to have such good fortune twice in one week, but when he'd returned the laptop Mr. Ballard had asked him to fix, before Jayden left to get his mother, Mr. Ballard said, "How long has it been?"

"What?" Jayden asked. He'd helped the exuberant older man with thinning black hair over the past several months with other small tasks, but he'd never asked him questions about his personal life. They usually discussed technology.

Mr. Ballard leaned back in his bed. He also had a small table in the room but rarely sat at it. "Since you've been inside?"

Jayden hesitated, feeling this throat tighten. He never sat down in Mr. Ballard's room unless invited but in shock he slowly sunk into the empty seat. How could he have found out? Not only had his case not be exciting enough to cause much of a stir in the local paper or online, but due to an error by the court reporter he'd been called *Jordan* Cassell (and like bad code it had been copied and pasted on other sites) so any mention of the case online would be under that name, rather than his own.

The man waved his ringed hand, a gold band from his alma mater catching the light. "It's okay. It's been thirty years for me. Embezzlement then fraud. I learned my lesson the second time."

Jayden folded his arms. "It's been nearly two years."

"Not long, huh? Finding it hard to get work?"

Yes, harder than he thought it would be. He wanted to tell him who he used to be. That he'd hoped that with his skills he would have managed to find something above minimum wage, but hadn't. If he hadn't lost his room at the boarding house because he had to help his mother with her health costs, he'd have made the low paying job work.

He'd kept his secret by knowing where to park his car at night so the cops wouldn't hassle him; he had rented a small storage locker so the interior of his car stayed clean; and knew where to wash up and get a meal when desperate. He shrugged. "I get by."

"You'll never get out of the hole you're in doing crap jobs. Don't let anyone fool you. The harder you work, the less you get paid. You've got to be smart and use your head, not your body. That's your problem. People are going to look at a big guy like you and peg you, but I can tell you're a smart guy. Where did you learn so much about computers?"

Jayden briefly told him about his background. Mr. Ballard nodded. "Why aren't you in that field now?"

"Thought I'd have something when I got out, but it fell through and—"

"And people feel uneasy working with an ex-con?"

Jayden nodded.

"Well, being one myself, I don't mind. I own a company that could use you. Ever thought of being an IT consultant?"

He shook his head.

"I'm getting out of this place in a week. It's not prison, but it's certainly not home, and I'm looking forward to going home." He grabbed his wallet from the side table and pulled out a business card then held it out to Jayden. "Come to this address next Tuesday and ask for me. Your days of crap jobs are over."

Jayden took and held onto the card as if it were a lifeline. It was the promise of a new life. One where he could use his skills and be the man he used to be. He almost told his mother about the possibility, but decided to wait. He wouldn't say anything until it was finalized, but things were looking up. His mother had a new place to stay and soon he'd have another way to make income. Soon a place like this wouldn't seem so out of reach.

"It's okay," he told his mother, sliding his hand over the soft blue bed sheet. He briefly envied her having such a nice place to sleep. He'd sleep on the floor if he could.

"Did you lie to me?"

He turned sharply to her. She stood in front of the spacious closet. "What?"

"Nicole doesn't really need the money, does she?"

He shrugged, hoping to appear nonchalant. "That's what she said. It's not for me to question her."

"I'm sure she could make money renting this place out to travelers and just fit me in the cupboard."

He closed the closet door. "Right now this place is yours. Don't worry."

"When will you let me see where you're staying?"

Why? It's parked outside. "Soon."

Dionne walked over to the bouquet of flowers and smelled it. "Nicole is very kind." She sent him a look. "I like her."

Jayden frowned and shook his head. "Don't start, Mum."

"If she knew who you really were—"

"You wouldn't have a place to stay right now."

"You weren't always struggling like this. You used to have a great job—"

He rubbed the back of his neck and sighed. "That was a long time ago."

"Not that long. And she—"

"She's not for me. Do you need anything else?"

"No." She walked over to the bed. "I'm going to take a nap."

He nodded. She was upset with him, but he was getting used to it. He wasn't going to let her think there was any chance he could start a relationship with Nicole.

He closed the front door behind him, making sure it was locked, before he headed to his car.

"You're leaving already?"

He turned and saw Nicole coming from the main house. "Mum's taking a nap."

"I was going to invite you both in for tea. But you'll do." She turned and went back inside before he could refuse her. He glanced at his car, pensive. In seconds he could be inside and gone. Then he'd call her and tell her he'd had an emergency. And then...

"Are you glued in place?" Nicole called out to him.

If only it were that simple. He sighed and turned to her. "Are you sure my car's safe?"

She grinned knowing he was joking. It wasn't that kind of neighborhood. "The tires might be taken, but the body should be safe."

"You're obsessed with my body, aren't you?"

She winked. "You're catching on."

CHAPTER FOURTEEN

He knew she was teasing him, but it didn't stop him from noticing her body in return. His eyes skimmed her jeans to notice her shapely legs and backside and the lovely curve of her hips as she walked through the front door. He knew if he followed he was courting trouble, but he'd come this far. One date down and two to go.

He could handle tea.

Jayden stepped inside the ceramic tiled foyer, greeted by the scent of something with cinnamon baking in the oven, then followed the glossy hardwood flooring to the sitting area where he saw Nicole. On the coffee table sat a tray with cheese, fresh fruit, vegetables and crackers.

He stepped back when he felt something damp press against his trouser leg. He glanced down and saw a little Pomeranian sniffing him.

"Come here, Coco," Nicole said.

The dog turned and sat by its owner. Jayden sat in

front of her then looked at the tea tray. "You didn't have to do all this."

"I know. Want me to pour?"

"Sure."

She lifted the teapot. "Coco wants to show off for you. Do you mind?"

He glanced at the little dog whose gaze seemed fixed on him. "Uh, no."

"Go on, girl."

The little dog walked up to him, turned in a circle twice then rested its head on its two front paws by way of a bow.

"She's showing off because she just came from the groomers," Nicole said.

He nodded. "Cute."

"I know the trick isn't amazing, but it seems to make her happy? Cream? Sugar?"

"Both please."

Nicole sent him a look, her gaze falling to his hands gripped in his lap. "It's okay, you can pet her. She doesn't bite."

Jayden knew it was an invitation to be friendly with the animal, but he still felt awkward. He hadn't grown up with furry animals like this, preferring reptiles, and most people seemed to keep their animals close to them when he walked by. He cleared his throat, bent down and gave the little dog two quick pats on the head. "Good girl."

Nicole jumped up. "Oh... I've got something warming in the oven. I'll be back in a second." Coco trotted behind her.

Jayden grabbed a cheese slice then took a sip of his

tea. He was on his second sip when he heard a squeak next to him. He looked down and saw a rubber chicken. Coco looked up at him. He looked away, wondering what was taking Nicole so long. He heard the squeak sound again. He looked down. Coco looked up at him.

"Are you making that sound?"

The dog picked up the toy and dropped it making the toy squeak.

Jayden frowned. "I'm sorry. I don't get it."

Coco picked up the toy then dropped it.

"Aw, that's so cute," Nicole said coming into the room followed by the scent of fresh banana bread. She set the bread on the table. His stomach growled. He cleared his throat hoping she hadn't heard it. "She wants you to play with her."

"Play with her?"

"Yes."

He picked up the toy then dropped it.

Nicole laughed. "No, she wants you to throw it."

"Oh." Jayden picked up the toy and threw it across the room with such force that it flew across the room bounced against the wall and hit a wooden statue, knocking it to the ground.

He swore. "Sorry, I didn't mean—"

Nicole got up before he could and quickly replaced the statue while Coco retrieved her toy.

He stood. "I should go. Sorry, Coco."

Coco placed the toy by his shoe.

"She's giving you another chance."

"I don't know what I'm doing." And he felt out of place in this beautiful home, with this beautiful woman and a cute little dog that wanted to play with him. He shoved his hands in his pockets.

Nicole nodded to the couch. "Sit down."

"I really should—"

"I think you chipped my statue. Do you know how much it costs?"

He swore.

"I'll forget the price, if you sit down."

He reluctantly did.

Nicole sat down beside him. He tried not to notice her thigh brushing his, although the rest of his body did. "Now toss the toy in the air not too high and see what she does."

Jayden did and to his surprise Coco jumped up in the air and caught it. "Wow, for a little dog she can really soar."

"It's her favorite game."

He did it again. And again. And again.

Nicole laughed. "I think it's your new favorite game too."

"What else can she do?"

Nicole shrugged. "That's about it."

Jayden lightly patted the little dog twice on the head again. "Clever girl."

"She likes you. She's not made of glass. You can really pet her you know."

"She's so small I wouldn't want to hurt her."

Nicole took his hand and slid it through Coco's soft fur. "Easy. See?"

It wasn't easy. It wasn't easy having Nicole lay her hand over his, and slid his hand through Coco's silky soft fur. Coco rolled on her back.

"Coco, stop flirting," Nicole said.

Jayden rubbed her tummy. "You'd better be careful someone could steal her."

"She's usually more vicious. You're lucky she likes you."

He couldn't imagine this cute little dog being vicious with anyone.

Nicole handed him a wet cloth. "For your hands."

He nodded. "Thanks." He cleaned his hands then reached for the bread and took a bite. It was moist, sweet and warm.

Oh so warm.

Like home. He lifted his tea cup and wrapped his hands around it letting the heat seep to his fingers, heat his palms. He wanted to keep this warm feeling when the chilly night fell and he was alone in his car again. Tiny comforts others took for granted were a luxury to him.

He inhaled the scent of spiced black tea and took another slice of banana bread adding a slice of cheese. He leaned against the soft give of the sofa, heard the sound of warm air coming through the vents.

He saw the throw on the back of Nicole's couch and half wanted to take it or ask to borrow it for a couple days, but he turned his gaze away. He'd learned to live in the moment in order to survive and he would now. He took another sip of the tea letting it warm him inside as he watched the steam rise up.

He shouldn't have come inside. Leaving would be hard.

"Why didn't you tell me you were hungry?"

"What?" Jayden asked then noticed half of the bread was gone. He silently swore. "I was focused on moving Mum and lost track of time and—"

"You don't have to explain. Let me make you something else and I'll wrap the rest of the bread to take home with you."

He wanted to reject her kindness, but she didn't give him a chance to as she dashed into the kitchen. Jayden hung his head.

Coco lightly tapped him with her paw and when he looked at her she rolled on her back.

"Really? You want more?" He bent down and stroked her. "I think I can manage that."

He probably imagined it but the dog looked like she was smiling and for some reason the thought of that made him happy. Her absolute trust and joy was intoxicating. He hesitated then picked her up. "Does your mum let you on the couch?" He placed the dog on his lap. "I don't think she'd mind this." He scratched her behind the ears.

Nicole stood in the entryway and looked at Jayden amazed. No one had ever been so entranced with her dog before, but Jayden looked completely smitten and it was funny to see. He was so large and yet tender with Coco and Coco seemed to know her power over him. If Coco had been another woman Nicole would have been jealous.

Nicole walked into the room carrying a large brown bag. "You've never had a pet before?"

He paused as if caught doing something wrong. Coco turned and licked his hand as if telling him to continue.

Nicole took a seat beside him, again brushing her thigh against his. "I'm only curious."

Jayden continued stroking the dog, resisting the urge to move closer. "I told you. I had a turtle."

"Besides a turtle."

"Do spiders count?"

"I suppose. Did you name it?"

He blinked. "I called him Spider. I didn't see the point in giving him a name he wouldn't respond to. Besides, I didn't want to grow too attached."

"Why not?"

He shrugged. "I was ten. It seemed like a good idea at the time."

"Most ten year olds would want a dog."

"True."

"You didn't like having pets?"

"Losing Lucy was hard."

"You named a turtle Lucy?"

He nodded.

"What happened to her?"

Jayden bit his lip then sighed. "I had an aunt come and visit from the country who loved to cook."

Nicole covered her mouth already guessing what he was about to say.

"She surprised the family with turtle soup."

"I'm so...that's awful. You poor thing."

Jayden shrugged and scratched Coco under the chin. Lucy should have been his first lesson. He'd gotten too attached to Monica too and losing her had hurt even more. They'd dated for two years. He'd planned to spend his life with her and they were only months from getting married before...

Nicole playfully nudged him. "You're spoiling her."

He looked down at Coco. "She's sweet. I've never had anything like me this much before."

"I like you." She whispered, her breath warm, her soft lips brushing his ear.

He sent her a long look. "You hardly know me."

She nodded to the dog. "Neither does Coco."

He held her gaze and deepened his voice. "Would you like me to stroke you?"

Nicole crossed her legs and leaned towards him. "Where would you start?"

His gaze skimmed over her form. *Everywhere.* He would cover her skin with long, languid strokes, making her body warm then hot. But he didn't say anything. Instead he set Coco on the ground and stood. "I really should go."

"Fine," she said with amusement as if she already knew what he'd been thinking. "Here's your lunch. We'll continue this conversation on our second date."

"Where do you want to go? Because I know another diner if—"

A sly smile spread on her lips. "I'll let you know."

CHAPTER FIFTEEN

He wouldn't sleep with her.

God how he wanted to sleep with her.

He wouldn't touch her.

He wanted to touch her all over real slow. He wanted to touch her everywhere. He wanted her to touch him. To feel him. To let her fingers slid down and wrap around his hard...

Jayden squeezed his eyes closed. He lay back in the driver's seat with his coat draped over him. He couldn't sleep. He couldn't stop thinking about Nicole. It didn't help that his car smelled like the banana bread she'd given him. And banana bread made him think of warm ovens and that got him thinking about warm bodies. And then in his mind Nicole was a warm—no hot—oven that he'd like to slide inside. And he thought of oven mitts for protection, and bread rising, slowly lifting to a peak.

It was a cool night and he felt hot. He wanted her so bad. *He wanted to feel again. As much as it would hurt him and he knew it would hurt. It had been too long since touch had been a pleasure. Nicole couldn't be the first after all these years. He couldn't give her that kind of burden. He'd be too hungry. He'd devour her. And he wanted to devour ever last inch.*

He squeezed his eyes harder and groaned. He could not sleep with her. Not yet. He'd wait to meet Mr. Ballard again and get his first cheque then maybe he could pull this off. With a job and a new place he could be the man Nicole thought he was.

But not yet. That had to be his rule.

CHAPTER SIXTEEN

When she was a child, Nicole had once found an empty cocoon. She'd tenderly carried it home and stared at it for days wondering what kind of butterfly had emerged from it. Others would have thought it was ugly, but she'd thought it one of the prettiest things she'd ever seen. Jayden's mother reminded her of it for some reason. A hollow shell of something. As if something beautiful had once resided inside but had left her. Her brown eyes seemed lost, her voice as fragile as butterfly wings.

She felt if she moved too fast or spoke too loud she'd frighten her. She couldn't understand how she'd made it into her mother's raucous inner circle, but she may be of stronger stuff than she appeared to be.

Dionne Cassell had been staying at the cottage a few days before she invited Nicole over for tea.

Nicole looked at the pitiful spread pleased they were alone, with only the sound of the TV in the background.

Her aunt would have noticed that the biscuits were a little burnt, her mother would notice the apple slices were uneven and when Nicole peeked inside the teapot, after Dionne had added boiling hot water, the tea looked a little too watery. But Nicole appreciated the effort. "This is too much."

Dionne didn't think it was enough. She knew that Ernestina's daughter was used to finer things and she was terribly out of practice, but she hoped to get the younger woman to open up to her. She wanted to learn more about her so that she could help her son win her over.

"I don't get to entertain much," Dionne said and started to pour the hot tea then she heard a familiar voice on the TV. Her heart constricted. She turned and saw his face. Her mouth went dry. She jumped when she heard a shout.

Dionne turned back to Nicole and saw that she'd poured the tea on Nicole's arm instead of in the teacup. Nicole cradled her arm against her chest.

Dionne looked at the burn horrified. "I'm so sorry. I—"

"It's okay," Nicole said quickly rushing over to the sink to run cold water on the burn.

"I'm...I'm sorry."

"It was a simple accident. Do you have a sterile bandage somewhere?"

"I-I-I don't know."

"It's not a problem. I have some at my place." She left.

Dionne followed then stopped when she saw Jayden driving up.

Jayden braked to a stop, kicking up gravel, when he saw his mother waving her hands with tears streaming down her face. He'd come to surprise her and see how she was settling in, but had been surprised instead. He put the car in park and jumped out. "Mum, what happened?"

She pressed her hands together. "I messed up again. I'm so sorry."

"What happened?"

"It's all my fault."

He took a deep breath. He rested his arm around her shoulders and led her back inside the cottage. "Tell me what happened."

"I didn't mean to." She sat down and pointed to the kettle. "I heard your brother's voice then saw him on TV and got distracted. I'm so sorry."

"What did you do?"

"I burned her. I burned Nicole. I was pouring and I wasn't paying attention."

He softly swore. They'd scheduled a date for tonight. "Where is she now?"

Dionne covered her face. "It shouldn't have happened. It shouldn't be this way. You should talk to him."

Jayden sighed. He couldn't tell her that he had talked to him and the conversations hadn't been good. "He won't talk to me. I've made my choice and he's made his. That's the end of it. Now where is Nicole?"

"She went to the main house to get a bandage. Tell her I'm sorry."

He patted his mother on the shoulder then hurried to

the main house. He knocked then tried the knob, which easily turned in his hand. He walked inside. "Nicole?"

"I'll be right there."

"Where are you?"

"I'm looking for a bandage. Can't remember where I put them."

"Where are you?"

She poked her head out of the bathroom. "Here."

Jayden walked in, saw the burn on her arm and swore. It was ugly, purple and starting to blister. "We have to take you to the hospital."

"No, I can take care of this myself. With a bandage and some Tylenol I'll be fine."

"They'll be able to—"

"Is the hospital your solution for everything?"

"In this case yes. It could get worse and my mother will never forgive herself. Come on. We'll take your car."

CHAPTER SEVENTEEN

A second degree burn.

She'd been lucky. If Nicole hadn't moved as quickly as she had, the damage could have been worse. The ER doctor cleaned the burn and wrapped it up and prescribed an antibiotic. When Jayden left to call his mother and reassure her, the nurse, a heavyset man with a silver mustache, lowered his voice and said, "Is there anything you want to tell us?"

Nicole looked down at her bandaged arm with regret. "I hope this doesn't leave a scar."

"It shouldn't if you follow the instructions." He hesitated. "Is there anything *else* you want to say? Anything...private."

"I'm sorry?"

"I remember you coming in only a month ago with another injury."

"It's really nothing," Nicole said quickly. "I'm fine, truly. But I appreciate you asking."

The nurse sent Jayden a nervous look before he turned back to her. "There are phone numbers you can call at all times. And apps that—"

"I have nothing to fear from him," Nicole said with a smile. "It truly was an accident. Thank you."

But she felt shaken. Something about Dionne bothered her, she was so absent minded somehow and the way she'd gasped when she'd looked at the TV.

And the words of the nurse bothered her too. It reminded her of something else, something bad, but she couldn't put her finger on it yet.

She searched her mind as Jayden led her through the hospital lobby to the exit, desperate to find the cause of the unsettling feeling when she heard someone call out "Professor?"

Jayden spun around then a big smile crossed his face. She'd seen that unguarded expression once on his face when she'd asked him out. That expression had been one of amusement. This was one of joy.

The skinny, black guy with a stud earring looked happy too and they embraced like long lost brothers. "I thought it was you, man."

It was a funny sight. For a moment the skinny guy seemed to disappear in Jayden's big embrace before reappearing again when Jayden released him. Neither seemed to care how odd their reunion looked.

"Nicole," Jayden said by way of introduction, "this is Francis. Francis, Nicole."

"Nice to meet you," Nicole said, shaking the man's outstretched hand.

"This your woman?" Francis asked with a playful grin.

"We're just friends," Jayden said.

Francis rubbed his hands together and licked his lower lip in a teasing leer. "We can be friends too."

Jayden rested a large hand on the man's thin shoulder. "I'm friendly enough for two of you."

Francis laughed. "I hear you, Professor."

"You didn't tell me you're a professor," Nicole said.

Jayden shook his head. "Because I'm not."

"But you used to be?"

He hesitated. "Not quite. I—"

"He's being humble," Francis said. "Best teacher I've ever had. He wasn't a real professor but it's what we called him. Cardoza gave him that name." He patted Jayden on the back with affection. "This guy knew sh—I mean stuff I'd never heard about, man. Stuff I thought he was making up. And he could remember things like nobody I knew. When he got library privileges you would have thought—"

"We're running late," Jayden cut in, "and I need to take her back home. But where are you staying?"

Francis looked a little confused then nodded. "Right, right. You're busy. I'm staying at my sister's place." He gave the address. "And I even got a phone too." He pulled it out to show it off. "Can you believe that? I used to say—"

"What's your number?"

Francis again paused uncertain. He glanced at Nicole before he gave Jayden the number.

Jayden took the man's hand and held it, warmth in his

voice when he spoke. "Really good to see you again. You'll hear from me." He turned and headed for the exit.

He stayed silent on the drive back while Nicole's mind swirled with questions that she kept to herself.

"We'll take a rain check on today," he said walking her up to her front door once they'd reached her house.

She opened the door and turned to him surprised. She had great plans for tonight and a great little black dress to match. "But I'm okay."

He shoved his hands in his pockets. "You're taking medication. You should rest."

All he had were excuses. Their second date was hours from now, there was no reason to cancel except that he didn't want to see her. He was more eager to reunite with Francis.

She should let him out of his misery. Dating her was clearly torture. She looked at him. She always liked looking at him (briefly imagining he'd wrapped his arms around her the way he'd hugged his friend, except he'd hold her longer and tighter) but now she looked at him with a critical eye.

He always had his hands in his pockets and kept his distance from her. Instead of making him seem smaller, he seemed even bigger. She didn't know why he did it. She remembered a kid from when she was in elementary school who'd always had his hands in his pockets and his shoulders hunched up close to his ears as if he wanted to be as small as possible so that no one would notice him.

Unfortunately, he was always noticed by the tallest kid who kicked him every chance he could. Nicole had once told the bully to cut it out then his adoring girlfriend spilled her orange juice all over Nicole's science project. And nothing changed.

But the grateful boy gave her a tiny bag of candy hearts. He avoided her gaze for the next couple of weeks until his family moved and she always hoped that at his next school he was treated better. But Jayden didn't remind her of that boy. He didn't look like someone who'd been bullied. He looked like a man who'd been bowed down by life, but was fighting to still stand tall, by keeping people at a distance.

Some people.

He seemed close to Francis, but he kept his distance with her.

Twice, on their first date, while taking a brief walk after the diner, walking along the pavement, she tried to loop her arm through his, but he easily moved away. The first time she thought it was an accident; the second time she got the hint. The sign was: Stay away from me.

Perhaps he didn't like women or he just didn't like her. If she hadn't asked him for three dates he wouldn't have volunteered. It was pathetic on her part. He only cared about his mother.

Don't even smell it. That's what her aunt had warned her when Nicole had first looked at him. Damn, Aunt Cleo had really been right.

He was fun in spite of his quirks (on top of not liking being touched, his gaze didn't stay in one place long; he was always surveying his surroundings, and at least twice she could be sure he was going to ask "Are you alright?") but he was not for her. It was time to move on.

"Listen, Jayden. You don't have to—"

"I really don't want to go," he said with an emphasis she hadn't heard before. This time when she met his gaze it wasn't just intense. It burned, holding her still, sending goose bumps along her skin. "But I have to. Go inside and sleep. I'll check in on you when I can." He kissed her before he jumped in his car and drove away.

Leaving her lips burning.

The camera loved him.

And Brian Cassell loved the camera. He also loved the rush of getting to a story. Of uncovering things. It had been a dream of his and he'd fought his way to make it come true. Now he had a popular local TV show called "Georgia Secrets" that helped reunite loved ones after painful separations. The irony that he was estranged from his own family wasn't lost on him.

Brian sat in his den finishing his favorite candy apple flavored e-cigarette while he watched the latest promotional campaign for season five of his show. He watched two old friends embrace. It made him feel good to help others. It had only been by luck that his family's stain hadn't impacted his career as much as it could have. It had been good that he'd left Tennessee way before anything really ugly had happened.

He heard his wife's heels as she walked into the den. He pulled his gaze away from the flat screen. His wife

Carla also looked good on TV or anywhere for that matter. He'd seen a picture of her online featuring rising marriage therapists and knew he'd wanted to meet her. It hadn't taken him long to convince her to marry him. After four years together she still looked gorgeous even when she was annoyed. Like she did now. "What did I do this time?"

"She called my phone again."

Carla didn't need to tell him who "she" was. He'd been avoiding his mother's calls for years. He couldn't remember how she'd gotten his wife's number. Some relative perhaps. "Did you answer?"

"No."

"Then why are you telling me about it?" he asked, bored.

"I think you should at least listen to her message."

He lifted his brows in surprise. "She left a message?"

"Not this time but—"

"Then there's nothing to discuss."

"Don't you feel bad?"

He sniffed. "You mean like survivor's guilt?"

She frowned. "That's not funny. I think you should—"

He waved his finger at her. "Stick with marriage counseling, darling. Family dynamics are out of your reach."

She crossed the room and sat on his lap. "I know it hurts you." She slid an arm around his shoulders, bringing her body close. "I only want to help."

He wrapped his arms around her waist. She smelled good and felt even better. "My mother is dangerous and staying away is the only way to survive. Look what happened to my brother." He looked around the spacious room with designer furniture. "Do you think you'd be living like this if I kept that woman in my life?"

"But she's your mother."

He sniffed and returned his gaze to the flat screen. "She stopped being that a long time ago."

He didn't like that his mother was getting to Carla, but she was crafty like that. Soon she'd make him the villain, but he didn't care. He had a life he would protect. His mother was not coming back in it.

He wished he could save his brother though, but it was too late for that. His brother's life had taken a turn neither of them would have expected.

He missed him. He hated that the most. He thought he'd get over it. He thought he could make himself forget Jayden. But he loved his brother too much even though he hated what he did. He hated the thought that he was still tied to his mother and didn't see what she was really like. How much real harm she'd caused.

When his brother had called him nearly two months ago, he'd wanted to ask him how he was doing, where he was staying. But instead his brother wanted him to look after their mother and that angered him. Jayden always put their mother's needs above his own. It had cost him everything.

But what Brian hated more was how much his brother's choice had cost him too.

~

DIONNE DIDN'T KNOW why she kept hoping Brian would forgive her. But she needed his help. She needed a way to fix things. She didn't want Nicole to see her as a burden and think of tossing her out of the cottage. If Brian would let her stay a couple days with him then...

Dionne stared at the phone in her hand then set it on the coffee table. She'd cleaned up the tea spill, but her life couldn't be as easily dealt with.

Her younger son wouldn't even speak to her. The last day she'd seen him was at the trial where Jayden pleaded guilty.

She saw rage in his gaze.

Rage. Not at Jayden but at her.

That shouldn't be a sight any mother should see. Or remember when she closed her eyes at night. Dionne wrote him letters, they were all returned; she sent him emails likely never opened.

But how could she expect him to forgive her when she could barely forgive herself? Most days she wanted to turn the clock back and remember happier times. She wondered if she'd ever feel that kind of happiness again. If she even deserved to.

Their last book club meeting had made her believe that it was possible. She was happy for Ernestina's new happiness but also envied it. She didn't like living alone. She wanted to feel a man's touch.

And the other women in the book club understood, that was what really bonded them. Their book club was made up of divorcees and widows and two women who'd never married (although Dionne couldn't fathom how they'd managed that) and made her feel less alone and embarrassed about her desires.

With them she could admit that she liked being part of a couple. She liked going grocery shopping with someone and planning trips together.

Fortunately, she'd met someone new and they were taking it slow, but she knew that Jayden would be against it and she didn't want to upset him right now. She'd caused him enough trouble after busting her hip. But one day she'd tell him, let him know that he could trust her. This time around she knew the signs and if she got married again she had friends to help her stay safe.

Yes, marriage was the first thing she'd thought about when she'd met her new man.

She didn't like living alone, that's why she wanted to live with her son. To fill that empty space. To hear a man's footsteps, the scent of his aftershave. If she could prove she wouldn't be a burden maybe Jayden would change his mind and let her back into his life completely.

She knew, however, he was keeping her at a distance for another reason. She knew him too well to believe that his place was too small to accommodate her. He was hiding something and soon she'd find out what it was.

CHAPTER NINETEEN

In twenty minutes he'd smell like cigarettes and Georgia Brown, but he didn't care. Jayden set his glass down, licking the foam of the sweet yet mild brown ale from his upper lip and sat back satisfied. His back brushed against the black duct tape which covered a tear in the grey cloth couch. He didn't regret seeing Francis again or taking Nicole to the hospital (even though he'd had to drive her car to save his gas) or kissing Nicole on her doorstep before he'd left.

He hated leaving her though, but knew if he didn't leave, he'd get into deeper trouble.

Francis sat across from him and said something but his words were drowned out by the sound of the blender. Francis' mother stood in the kitchen mixing a green drink while his niece sat entranced in front of the TV watching a cartoon.

Francis turned to her annoyed and shouted, "Momma, do you have do that now?"

She pulled the cigarette from her mouth and shouted back, "I'm almost done, baby. You sure you don't want some?"

"I'm more than sure." Francis turned to Jayden and lowered his voice. "Tastes like grass and I'm not talking the kind you can smoke, man. I mean pulled from your lawn nasty." He nodded to the five brown boxes with the words VeggieLiteDrink stacked against the wall. "She and my sister are trying to sell it as a side business."

The whirring sound rose again then finally stopped. "You boys don't know what you're missing," Francis' mother said. She took a long drag of her cigarette before she crushed it in a nearby ashtray. "This is healthy stuff."

"He's not buying."

"I wasn't trying to sell him nothing," she said sounding hurt. "He could have had a free sample."

"Another time," Jayden said. He took another sip of his drink.

Francis leaned forward, eager to continue their conversation. "So let me get this right. Your woman doesn't know?"

Jayden licked his top lip. "I told you she's not my woman."

"But you want her to be."

Jayden took another sip.

"And she doesn't know nothing?"

Jayden shook his head and set his glass down. "Nope."

Francis rubbed his chin. "I know your momma needs a place, but that's a risk, man."

"I know."

"And it looks like she likes you. I mean you two being all 'friendly' and all."

Jayden couldn't stop a smile. "I like her too."

"Then you have to—"

"I might be able to make this work. I've got a job offer."

"That pays?"

"Of course it pays. If it didn't pay it would be volunteering."

Francis nodded slowly in understanding. "Yeah, right." He clapped his hands together, pleased. "See? There you go being all smart and sh—"

Jayden waved his praise away. "It's nothing."

"I want what's best for you, man. You know that, right? And I've got a few years on you too so I'll give you a little advice. You'd better tell her before she finds out from someone else and loses her mind. And I mean freaky. This one guy I knew...man...his girl went so freaky he had nightmares for days. I'm talking screaming fits and night sweats."

"Nicole isn't like that."

"Any woman is like that. One moment they're normal then— Boom! Crazy." He clasped his hands together. "The way I see it, if she can't take your past she doesn't belong in your future."

Jayden smiled, amused. "You're becoming a philosopher now?"

"Hey, I read all them books you told me to. I learned something."

"Glad to hear it. But don't worry about me. With a

good job and a nice place, I'll get her to understand the rest."

Francis shrugged. "Suit yourself, trying to reach for the stars, man. But if she doesn't work out, my cousin's got a sister named Kiki."

"Your cousin."

"What?"

"If your cousin has a sister, then she's also your cousin."

Francis paused, thoughtful. "Oh, yeah, that's true. I never thought about it that way 'cause she's his sister by marriage and if you saw what he looked like and what she looked like you'd know they ain't blood relatives and—"

Jayden shook his head. "Never mind."

"Anyway...what was I saying?"

"You were telling me about Kiki."

Francis snapped his fingers. "Right, anyway, she ain't picky about nothing and nobody. A man gots to get his needs met, right? So if you want her number—"

"I'll let you know."

"You do that. How's your momma's health?"

He sighed. He'd told Francis a lot about his mother, since he'd asked about the picture of her Jayden had posted on his cell wall. "Getting better. I'll have you over soon. Knowing all you did for me she'd like to meet you."

Francis suddenly looked embarrassed. "I didn't do nothing. We helped each other out. How's your brother?"

Jayden took a long swallow of his beer then lied. "Still haven't spoken."

"His loss. I've got five sisters." His lifted his glass as if in a toast. "I'll take whatever brother comes my way."

CHAPTER TWENTY

She nearly slammed the door in his face, but resisted. Instead, Nicole rested her hip against the doorframe and stared at Jayden as he stood on her doorstep. It had been three days since she'd last seen him. He'd sent her a text, left a message, but he'd stayed away. In those three days she'd had another nightmare she couldn't remember (with no hand to hold and deep voice to soothe her) and, worse, she had missed him.

"You took your time. After you drove my car, do you know how long it took me to readjust the driver's seat so that my feet could touch the pedals?"

He bent down and stroked Coco. "I've been busy. How are you doing?"

"My arm fell off," she said in a cool tone. "Can't you tell?"

He straightened and met her gaze. "I'm glad to see you're feeling better."

She looked down unable to meet his eyes. They were always her undoing. She was both happy and annoyed by the sight of him and didn't know what to do with her conflicting emotions. So she focused her gaze on his clothes and noticed his suit. It was the same one he'd worn on their first date. "Why are you all dressed up?"

"I've got a meeting with a client in a few hours. I thought I'd check on you first."

"Is it an important meeting?"

"Very. I'm hoping to get more business."

"Then you can't go dressed like that."

He looked down. "What's wrong with how I'm dressed?"

"Should I start with the jacket or the trousers?"

Jayden tugged on the lapel. "What's wrong with my jacket?"

"Aside from the fact that it hardly fits?"

He looked away embarrassed. "It'll do."

"No, it won't." She clicked her tongue irritated that she couldn't stay angry at him for long. Especially when he was clueless. "We have to go shopping. Relax, I'll pay and you can pay me back later."

An hour later, Nicole gave a low whistle of appreciation when Jayden stepped out of the dressing room wearing blue trousers, a single-breasted blazer, striped dress shirt and brown shoes. "Much better. Don't look at me like that, Brown Bear. You know you look good." She tugged on his collar. "Although we will need to get this tailored later. A man like you cannot pull clothes off the rack and expect them to fit perfectly."

Jayden told himself not to worry as each item was

rung up and the amount rose. He would be able to pay her back soon. When he'd spoken to him, Mr. Ballard had made his offer sound like a sure thing. Today they would finalize things and then he could treat Nicole to something special for their second date.

"You've got to explain something to me," Nicole said as Jayden put his old clothes in the backseat of his car. She leaned against the passenger door with her arms folded and looked around at the other parked cars.

He closed the back door and looked at her. "What?"

"That kiss."

He feigned surprise, resting his hand on the top of the car. "What kiss? Did somebody kiss you?"

"Yes, this big brown bear."

He scratched his beard. "You should have fought him off."

"It happened too fast."

"Then maybe it wasn't really a kiss." A soft smile danced around his lips. "Maybe you imagined it."

"It wasn't my imagination. His lips touched mine."

"Hmm." He started to walk to the drivers' seat.

"I wasn't going to see him again, but then he did that."

Jayden paused and turned to her with genuine surprise. "Why weren't you going to see him again?"

"Because I wasn't sure he liked me."

He slowly walked back to her. "And you think the kiss means he likes you?"

"I might have to kiss him again to make sure."

He stood in front of her and trapped her in the circle of his arms, his hands on either side of her, resting against the hood of the car. "He can't let that happen."

Nicole swallowed. "Why not?"

"Because if he kisses you then he'll want to touch you."

"And that's a problem?"

He nodded and his voice deepened. "Because then he'll want to touch you even more."

"Is that the problem?"

He nodded again. "Because he doesn't want to sleep with you yet."

Nicole grinned. "I like that 'yet' bit."

"I thought you would." He pushed himself away from her. "So now you understand."

"One doesn't necessarily lead to the other."

"With me, it will." He walked to the driver's side and got inside.

"That won't be a bad thing," Nicole said, putting on her seatbelt. "Two adults who—"

He started the car. "I'm not sleeping with you." He turned to her. "I mean it."

Nicole held her tongue the rest of the drive, but when he drove up to her house she couldn't stand the silence any longer. "Come inside. I want to show you something."

Jayden looked at the clock.

Nicole knew his meeting was still two hours away, he had time but she wanted to reassure him so she said, "It won't take long."

He put the car in park and followed her inside. He

greeted Coco with a quick pat before he said, "What is it?"

Nicole closed the door behind him, patted Coco on the head before directing the little dog back to the living room with a flick of her wrist. She then stood, looked at Jayden and said, "One minute."

"What?"

"You let me touch you for one minute. That's the cost of this suit."

He folded his arms, widening his shoulders. "And if I don't?"

Nicole started to smile, unfazed. "Otherwise, Brown Bear, you take it off now and go back into your old one."

He narrowed his eyes. "Don't think I won't. I don't like blackmail."

She lightly touched the hem of his jacket and said in a soft voice, "You may not like that, but I know you like this suit. You look too good right now and you said this meeting was important."

"You don't know what you're asking."

"I'm asking to spend one minute with a man I like very much."

He bit his lip, his gaze sliding down her body. Everywhere his eyes landed grew hot.

"Jayden?" she asked unable to stand his silence.

His voice deepened but he didn't lift his gaze. "I heard you."

"Then what's your answer?"

He didn't move. She saw his Adam's apple bob up and down as he swallowed. "Go ahead," he said. "I'll give you a minute." His gaze met hers. "Just mind the suit. It's costing me a lot."

Nicole's heart pounded sensing the challenge. "I'll be very gentle," she said, but her mind raced. She'd gotten him to do what she wanted and now she felt shy. How should she touch him? Where should she touch him? Why didn't he like to be touched? Why couldn't he be like a normal man? But then she realized that was why she liked him. He was like no one she'd ever met before. She liked her big, brown bear. A man who could be both cuddly and fierce. Was she being unfair to him? If he didn't want to do this, she shouldn't force him.

"Have you changed your mind?" he asked.

"Yes."

"I haven't."

She met his dark, compelling eyes. Permission. That's what she'd needed from him. Being with him like this felt so strange but also exciting. She flexed her hand then reached for his shirt.

"Stay above the waist," he growled.

She sighed. "I haven't even touched you yet."

"I'm giving you guidelines."

"That's disappointing."

He couldn't help a chuckle. "You do like playing with fire."

She looked him over. Where to start?

"Twenty seconds," he said.

"I do not have twenty seconds left."

"No, you've been wasting twenty seconds."

"It's only been ten and this is hard to do under pressure."

"You don't have to do this at all."

"You're right. But I want to." She really wanted to. If she could, she'd strip him down bare, inhale his sweet scent then wrap her body around him. Instead she pressed her lips against his neck then licked his skin with her tongue.

Jayden jerked back and covered his neck, staring at her wide eyed. "What the hell was that?"

"My minute isn't up yet. You said I could touch you."

"With your *hands*."

"You weren't specific."

"I am now."

She slowly licked her lower lip and held his gaze. "You didn't like it?"

He held her gaze for a long moment then whispered in a low growl, "Too much."

He pulled her into his arms and covered her mouth with his own.

Nicole's thoughts went from spinning into overdrive. All her senses came alive. To say that he kissed her would be too tame a description. He possessed her mouth like a pirate seizing a treasure. It was wild, hungry, primal.

He drew away first and Nicole cried out in dismay. One kiss like that wasn't enough. It was like only tasting a dot of whipped cream on the tip of your finger. He was sweet and spicy at the same time. Sexy and intoxicating. She hadn't expected that. Who was this man?

She grabbed the front of his shirt before he could turn away from her. "Jayden, I—"

He removed her hand and smoothed down his shirt. "I'd better go." He turned and opened the door.

"Come back tonight. Tell me how the meeting went."

He headed out the door. "I can tell you over the phone."

She hooked the back of his collar with her finger, stopping him. "I'd prefer you tell me in person." She got on her tip toes and whispered in his ear, "I'll make it worth the drive."

CHAPTER TWENTY-ONE

Jayden stared at the receptionist unable to believe his ears. "I'm sorry?"

"Mr. Ballard unexpectedly passed away two days ago. I'm sorry. We're really overwhelmed right now and not taking any new clients. However, his son is handling most things. Can I refer you elsewhere? Would you like to speak with him?"

His heart fell. He stood in the lobby of Mr. Ballard's software company and couldn't move. "Uh, no. Thanks." Jayden doubted Ballard's son would be as open to hiring an ex-con as his father had been.

Jayden briefly closed his eyes feeling sick. How could he have died? He looked so healthy and he'd only seen him a week ago. What would he tell Nicole now? The only reason he'd kissed her the way he had was because he thought his life had changed. He had every intention of meeting her tonight and spending it with her. There was no way he could do that now.

But she would be expecting him, wanting him to tell her how his meeting went, and he couldn't stand her up again. Damn. He stood by the wall and stared down at the business card that had given him so much hope. He'd quit his job at the warehouse, but the manager liked him and said he was welcome back if he wanted.

He didn't want to go back. Mr. Ballard had opened a new desire in his heart. Nicole had too. But he didn't know what to do about it.

"I'm sorry, but Mr. Ballard passed away," he heard the reception say to someone else. Jayden glanced up and saw an unstylish woman in a blue suit with a ramrod-straight stance. "And we're not taking any new projects."

The woman bristled. "But he told me to come here specifically because of a special project."

"I don't know about that. If you leave a message, I can let his son get back to you in a couple of days."

"I don't *have* a couple days," the woman said in a tight voice.

Jayden stepped forward, sensing an opportunity. "I think I can help you." He rested a hand on his chest. "I'm Jayden Cassell. I'd spoken with Mr. Ballard about assisting him on expanding into IT analysis."

The woman looked him over and he could tell from her gaze that his expensive new suit gave the right impression. "I'm getting my cards printed now," he continued eager to keep her interest, "but I can provide analysis, advice and solutions for your organization's needs. I can also improve your data or software system."

"We need help urgently."

"I can come today, if you want." He held his breath.

She nodded and said, "Follow me."

THREE HOURS later Jayden got into his car after solidifying his first deal. Now he was lying to three women: His mother, Nicole and now the manager of a small marketing firm. But if this project worked, the risk would be worth it. The troubles at the company were minor so he could deal with them easily. It shouldn't take more than a couple of days. He would be paid half upfront; the rest when he finished the task.

He stared down at the cheque in his hand. His new life started now.

CHAPTER TWENTY-TWO

Nicole stared at Jayden with a series of questions in her gaze, but all she said as he stepped into the foyer was, "Did the suit work?"

Jayden took off his jacket and carefully hung it over a chair. "The suit worked."

"Are you coming here to thank me?"

He picked up Coco, who'd come to say hello, letting her lick his face as he undid his tie. "You asked me to come back."

"You're supposed to pretend that you wanted to."

He cradled Coco in the crook of his arm, sat on the edge of the couch and looked at her with a level gaze. "I don't have to pretend."

She cleared her throat. "I wasn't sure you'd come."

His gaze slowly traveled down her gold satin robe and bare feet. He noticed her gold painted toenails and couldn't help a grin. "You look certain to me."

"I've been wrong before."

He nodded and lowered his gaze to the floor. "I know. I wasn't sure I should do this." He set Coco on the ground and folded his arms. "I'm still not sure."

"I think you made the right decision."

The ghost of a smile danced around his lips. "Somehow I knew you would say that."

"And somehow I thought you'd look happier."

He met her eyes, his steady gaze bore into hers with intense expectation. "I'm very happy. I'm letting you set the pace." He knew that was the only way tonight would work. The moment he touched her, he wouldn't let go. He couldn't deny what he wanted. The more he stayed away, the more he wanted her. It was a craving that only seemed to grow. He had to be rational, sensible and that meant letting her take the lead so he wouldn't frighten her. He had to protect her and himself.

She turned. "Let's go."

He rose to his feet. "Where?"

She threw a sly smile over her shoulder. "You really have to ask that?"

"You have a lot of rooms. There's the living room and the dining room..."

She walked down the hall. "We're heading to the bedroom. I don't think the couch can hold us and I don't want to do it on the floor."

Jayden followed her to the bedroom then stopped in the doorway, his eyes falling on the large bed covered by a maroon bedcover. He hadn't been in a bed so long. The thought of sinking into a soft bed with Nicole's warm body wrapped around him was like a double aphrodisiac.

Nicole sat on the bed and looked at him, concerned. "Is something wrong?"

He took a cautious step forward. It was like walking into heaven. "Nice room."

"Thanks."

He was halfway through unbuttoning his shirt when he realized she hadn't moved. She sat on the edge of the bed watching him with her hands flat on either side of her. But he couldn't read her face. His heart started to race. Had she changed her mind? If so, he had to get out now because once he started, stopping would be impossible. He'd be like a raging river, he could feel his desire for her coursing through his veins. He glanced at the door.

"Don't stop," she said in a low voice.

"What?"

"Don't stop what you're doing. I like watching you undress."

"Really?"

She nodded. "I like watching you full stop."

Why? What did she see? His heart leapt and cracked at the same time. He wasn't who she thought; he could never be that man for her. "Listen—"

She held up her hand. "You don't have to talk, right now. Unless I make you nervous."

He removed his shirt. "I'm not nervous."

An impish grin touched her lips. "If you knew what was going on in my mind right now, you would be."

"Is that a warning?"

"Do you need help with your trousers?"

"I think I can manage on my own."

"I'm here to help if you want."

"What I want is to see you undressing too."

"I will." She tugged on her robe. "But it won't take as long."

"Is it just you underneath that?"

She tilted her head to the side and said, "Finish what you're doing and you'll find out."

"You're a strange woman," he said without judgment.

"Because I like watching you?"

He nodded. "That's one of the reasons."

"I can't help being curious. You did offer me your body once. Remember?"

"I remember."

"I want to see what you were willing to sacrifice back then."

Jayden walked over to the bed and stood in front of her. "It wouldn't have been a sacrifice."

She reached up and touched his chest, he winced. She pulled her hand away.

"How come it hurts when I touch you?"

He pulled back the covers, got in bed and slid underneath. "It's not you. It's a bad habit."

She stood up. "Bad breakup?"

"Hmm." That was the least of it.

"Bad breakups are always hard to get over. One day I hope you'll tell me about it."

If only it were that simple. It wasn't just a breakup, it was watching his life explode, leaving him shattered. He didn't want to feel again afterwards.

But Nicole was slowly putting the pieces back together, giving him hope. He couldn't afford hope but he was going to pay the price anyway.

He couldn't afford to break and shatter again. Staying broken kept his safe. Kept them both safe. But he didn't want to be safe tonight. He wanted to teeter on the edge. Look down over the cliff.

She stood beside his side of the bed and didn't move.

He frowned. "What's wrong?"

"I'm having trouble with my robe."

He knew she was lying. With one tug of the sash he could get it opened and in less than a second he could have it on the floor. The thought made him smile. "Let me help you," he said, playing along. He undid her robe then drew her down on the bed. "You're right. Undressing you was easy."

He took her hand and placed it against his chest again. There was a question in her gaze, but he kissed her as his answer. Yes, touch me. No matter how I react, it doesn't matter if I flinch or wince, or if it seems like it hurts I want you to touch me all over. I want to be with you. I didn't come here by mistake.

Don't reject me now.

He closed his eyes, heard the sound of the bed sheets brush against her skin then felt her warm body pressed against his. He opened his eyes and saw his angel again; the same one who'd rescued him at the rehabilitation facility. She'd rescued him from darkness. Tonight he didn't feel like a beast—an animal that had to hunt and scramble to survive. Tonight he was in a bed, not a makeshift one he had to find and create for himself, but a real one with soft sheets that smelled like lilacs, with a woman who hadn't turned him away. She'd chosen him.

He didn't know why, he didn't care why. She'd allowed him to be a man again.

He'd known hunger before. But never hunger like this. When their lips touched he felt like a man starved. She couldn't touch him enough, be close enough. *I will become the man you think I am.*

Nicole held him close. This was the feeling she'd been searching for all her life. She couldn't name it, it was too complicated to name, but she felt it throughout her body. Jayden didn't just want her; it wasn't just about her tight thighs and flat stomach. She didn't feel like an interchangeable doll. When he whispered her name, she knew he wanted her. Just her. No other woman.

And for a moment tears stung her eyes as the pain of hurt came flooding forward. She'd been hurt before, so very hurt but he didn't hurt her. She kept waiting for a greedy punishing kiss, grasping hands, selfish pleasure.

But every touch was like a benediction. He treasured her, cared for her. She almost felt worshiped. In return she worshiped him. No part of him frightened her. Not his size, not his intensity, not even his low grumble. Instead it excited her. Her breasts tingled against the feel of hair on his chest, when he entered her he freed a burst of sensations.

She'd teased him about offering his body as a sacrifice, but the true sacrifice was her heart. She'd given it to him freely without knowing it and had no way to retrieve it.

She couldn't lose him. She wouldn't lose him. *Please don't leave me. Tell me how to make you stay.*

One day he would welcome her touch without flinching, she'd help him heal from the woman who had broken his heart and show him that he could trust her.

Her moment with him was over too soon, just as his kiss had been. She wasn't sure she'd ever get enough of him. Not yet at least.

She sleepily watched him get dressed. "You don't have to go."

"I have an early morning tomorrow." He pulled on his shirt and started to button up.

"You look great in your suit, but I like you better naked."

"Go to sleep," he said with laughter in his voice.

"Kiss me goodbye."

He shook his head, his face growing serious. "No, I never want to do that."

"Goodbye doesn't mean forever."

"I'll kiss you good morning instead." He brushed his lips against hers before he left.

Nicole didn't fall asleep right away, the bed felt suddenly cold and empty without him. And when she did fall asleep she knew she was alone to fight the haunting nightmare that she still couldn't remember.

CHAPTER TWENTY-THREE

To him she was home. She was everything. His heart, his breath, his sanity. With her he could sleep. No matter how cold the night, thoughts of her warmed him. And in his dreams...she was the sun that rose and set in the distance. Magnificent and untouchable. The sound of her breathing helped to drown out the audible memory that kept him up most nights. The sound of other men—some wheezing, others swearing, a few praying-the *click* and *clank* sound of cell doors opening and closing.

But Nicole was his key to freedom.

He knew he had nothing to offer her. But his heart still beat for her as much as he wished it not to. As much as it hurt him.

Jayden drove around the dark, empty streets unable to stop thinking of her. He could have stayed, but leaving was his punishment. He didn't want to use her.

His love for her hurt every day that he lied to her. Pretending to be someone else. Someone he used to be. If only she had met him years ago he would have had a chance. But not now. Never now. She would reject him and he couldn't blame her. He barely recognized the man he had become. Plus, he had his mother to think of. He knew her situation was only temporary. He needed to keep her safe and if Nicole found out the truth about him she might toss his mother out too.

But just for a moment he dreamed that Nicole could love him back as the man he was now. That she could accept him. His past mistakes, his present regrets.

But no one had ever loved him like that before. He doubted there was a woman who could. It was too much to ask.

He slowed as a traffic light turned from yellow to red. Touching her, letting her touch him, was sweet torture. He should have kept his distance. Denied himself the temptation. But he had fallen. Completely. Fully. It was one of the few things he didn't regret because the memory was something that would sustain him. Remind him he was still alive, although most of the time he felt dead.

Why did she make him want to live? Want to dream? Want to be with her? No other person had managed that since his release. But there was something about her that briefly allowed him to delude himself into a future of happiness.

He saw the traffic light turn green and put his foot on the gas.

A future with her.

But he knew any thought of a future was a lie.

A lie he'd created.

But a lie he could make real. He just needed time, even though he knew time was running out.

CHAPTER TWENTY-FOUR

He never spent the night.

After nearly two months and the slow rising heat of a summer in Georgia she was beginning to take it personally. The first few times his reasons seemed fine, but now they felt like excuses. Reasons that he didn't want to spend any more time with her than was absolutely necessary. At one point she half expected him to leave money on the side table.

She knew he liked her. He said he was happy. Their relationship seemed solid. Even her sister Stephanie liked him. They'd gone out, as a couple on a double date, and except for Stephanie discovering that Jayden was the author of some white paper she'd read online about an exploitable flaw in a known software (which to Nicole's horror led to nearly a thirty minute discussion among the three of them that left her yawning with boredom) the evening had been a success. "Usually guys as smart as him aren't so personable," Stephanie told her the following day. "I wonder why he's no longer a cybersecurity researcher."

"I told you he lost his job. I think he prefers consulting anyway." That night had been the first time she'd heard that part of his past.

Stephanie sounded uncertain. "But still he...doesn't matter, I guess. He's a great guy."

Yes, he was a great guy. Nicole lay in bed as she remembered her sister's words.

He was a great guy who never spent the night. Tonight that would change. Before Jayden could roll out of bed, she saddled him. "Spend the night."

He looked up at her amused. "Why?"

"Why not?"

He easily lifted her off of him and sat up.

"Please."

He swung his legs over the side of the bed. "Does it really mean that much to you?"

She wrapped her arms around his waist to keep him from standing. He winced. It was quick and barely detectible but she'd seen it all the same. She was learning not to let his reaction bother her. His reactions were better than before. She pressed her lips against his back. "Pleaseeee, Brown Bear."

He grumbled something.

She rested her chin on his shoulder. "What was that?"

"I said I sleep better alone. It's not personal."

"Okay, that makes sense. People have different sleeping habits. How about you stay in the guest bedroom? That way we can have breakfast together?"

"If it's breakfast you want, I can come over early and—"

"What's wrong with staying in the guest bedroom?"

"I like sleeping in my own bed."

"You've never invited me to stay the night in your bed."

He opened his mouth and she slid an arm over his shoulder and let it settle on his chest. She drummed her fingers against it with impatience. "I know, I know, it's not personal."

He wrapped his hand around hers. "Right."

She sat back. "I'll take a sleeping bag."

He turned fully to her. "What?"

"We have fun together and then I'll sleep on the ground—"

His look turned hard. "That's out of the question."

"I'm trying to find a way for us to have a sleepover," she said in a coaxing tone. "Is that so bad? I'd like to wake up in bed with you with my hair all over and puffy eyes and smile 'good morning' and have breakfast with you. Is that so wrong?"

He rubbed his nose. "No."

"Fine. So what is it? A guest bed or a sleeping bag?"

He bit his lip. "I can't have you sleeping on the floor."

"My sleeping bag is really comfortable. It will be like camping."

"Give me another month then I'll spend the night."

"What's happening next month?"

He fell silent for a long moment before he smiled a secretive smile, kissed her tenderly on the lips then whispered, "I'll be waking up next to you."

CHAPTER TWENTY-FIVE

He made her feel so alive.

Dionne looked across the round table in the food eatery at her date, a shared plate of fried rice and dumplings between them, and felt proud to be with such a distinguished and handsome man. She sighed feeling guilty.

"I probably should tell Jayden about us," she said.

"Only if you want to," her date said. "It's your life. You can do with it what you like."

That wasn't true. She owed her life to Jayden, but couldn't tell anyone that without revealing too much. "He's a part of my life."

Her date covered her hand, his brown eyes warm. "I hope I can say the same one day too."

She hoped so too.

She hated keeping secrets from Jayden again. Especially one like this. She'd promised herself she never would. But the temptation had been too much and

Ernestina so persuasive. Dionne did want to have her own life and now that Jayden was with Nicole things should be fine. No one could fault her. She still had plenty of life left. She wanted this. Her own happiness. She deserved it.

Nothing could go wrong this time.

CHAPTER TWENTY-SIX

Coco never woke her.

So Nicole knew something was wrong, when the dog scratched at her blanket and yelped.

She turned on the lights and rubbed her eyes. "What is it?"

Coco walked out the bedroom door. When Nicole didn't follow her, she reappeared in the doorway and barked. Nicole grabbed her robe and followed the insistent dog to the front door. "We have an alarm system if you hear anything outside," Nicole mumbled when Coco scratched at the front door, wanting her to open it.

Nicole opened the door and the dog darted out and headed down the drive her little paws kicking up gravel. Nicole raced after her. Then she stopped when she saw Coco barking at a car.

A black car.

A black Lexus.

A very, familiar black Lexus. Parked at the end of her drive.

Nicole peaked inside the passenger window and saw Jayden sleeping in the driver's seat. She tapped on the window. He shot up then looked at her, his eyes wide; a swear word broke from his lips, muffled by the glass. He turned away and rested his head on the steering wheel.

She knocked on the window.

He straightened in his seat and lowered it.

Nicole rested her arms on the window frame. "Care to explain this?"

"I have to pick Mum up for an early appointment and didn't want—"

"Try another lie."

"Why would I lie?"

"Because if you needed to pick your mother up early, you could have stayed with me or her. Yet you chose to sleep in your car." She pointed to his chair. "Is this the comfortable bed you were telling me about?"

Jayden rubbed the back of his neck, miserable. "The truth is I'm between residences right now."

"Is that a fancy name for homeless?"

"If you like."

"How long?"

"Almost eight months."

"And your mother doesn't know?"

He narrowed his eyes. "Do you think I'd be sleeping out here if she did?"

"Don't get testy with me. I'm not the one trespassing."

"Trespassing?"

"This is my property. Did I give you permission to sleep at the end of my drive?"

He sighed. "Please give me permission to—"

Nicole turned and picked up Coco. "Shut up and come inside."

Minutes later they sat in the living room facing each other. Coco walked back and forth between them as if trying to ease the tension in the room. She'd lick Jayden's hand then walk over and nudge Nicole with her head. When that didn't work, she sat down in the middle, resting her head on her paws and sighing.

"When were you going to tell me?" Nicole finally said.

Jayden scratched his cheek. "'Never' sounded about good. I'm doing some consulting work but the projects are not regular enough for me to make any promises to you and—"

"You can stay here."

"Nicole."

"I will not have my boyfriend sleeping in his car. You don't have to share my bedroom. I told you I have an extra."

He shook his head with regret. "That's not going to work."

"Why not?"

He briefly looked down then lifted his head. "You don't know me well enough yet and I don't want you to have any regrets."

"Regrets? I've been sleeping with a guy who's been lying to me for *months* and you're now bringing up the subject of regrets?"

"I didn't expect it to get this far. Things were looking up when I..." He let his words fall away. "You're right. I shouldn't have done this to you. I'm sorry I lied."

She shook her head. "I need you to answer one question."

"Depends on the question."

"No," she shot back, "it depends on whether you want to continue seeing me or not."

He sighed. "What's your question?"

"Have you ever been in prison?"

He paused, his gaze darkened. "Why?"

"Yes or no?"

"What made you think of that?"

"Because I still have a feeling you're hiding something from me."

Jayden clasped his hands together. He was going to lose his angel tonight. He shouldn't have parked his car in her drive, but it had seemed convenient at the time. He'd gotten tired of driving around at night looking for a place to park.

He glanced at the little dog. If it hadn't been for Coco he would have gotten away with it.

He ran a tired hand down his face suddenly feeling exhausted. Beaten. Tonight was nobody's fault but his own. He wanted to tell her that he'd hoped to get a small apartment next month. Big enough for both him and his mother. That he wanted to spend the night with her and wake up with her in the morning.

That he could whip eggs like a master chef. His father had taught him that. He'd tell her how his father used to make a spicy spinach omelet and he'd draw a smile on it using red hot sauce. They'd sweat their way through breakfast with smiles. He wondered if Nicole knew how to make omelets.

But no, it didn't matter.

He'd lied to her. He wouldn't lie anymore. He met her gaze and prepared for the end. "Yes."

She nodded. "For what, then?"

"Attempted murder."

CHAPTER TWENTY-SEVEN

Nicole didn't blink and she didn't move. "Attempted murder?"

He nodded.

"Care to elaborate? Or do you want me to fill in the blanks?"

"It was my stepfather. He touched my mother one too many times and I wanted to stop him." Jayden shrugged. "So I did. End of story."

"'Touched' sounds like an understatement."

He shrugged again.

"There are other ways to handle domestic disputes."

He nodded slowly. "So I've been told. I lost my temper and I wouldn't do it again but I did my time."

"How long?"

"I got ten but served four."

"Good behavior?"

He shrugged. "Something like that." He bit his lip. "You have nothing to be afraid of. I'd never hurt—"

"I'm not afraid." Nicole squeezed her eyes shut and covered her face. "I'm shocked, I'm angry, I'm confused," she let her hands fall and looked at him, "but not afraid." She threw her head back and laughed without humor. "Aunt Cleo is going to love this. She knew you were hiding something. I guess I didn't break my pattern of bad choices after all."

Jayden stood. "My mother doesn't need to suffer because of this. Let her stay a couple more weeks and—"

"No."

His heart grew cold. If she threw his mother out tonight, he didn't know how he'd explain it. But Nicole had a right to her anger; he knew what betrayal felt like. "Okay, please just let her sleep through the night and I'll get her in the morning so—"

Nicole lifted up one of the couch pillows and hit him with all her might. "I hate you! I hate you so much Jayden Cassell. I hate you standing there and expecting me to be a coldhearted bitch who'd toss your mother out into the cold because I was mad at you." Tears filled her eyes and her voice as she hit him again. "I hate you for not trusting me to understand your situation." She gripped the front of her nightgown. "I hate you for hurting me like this." She tossed the pillow on the ground. "But as much as I hate you right now. I hate myself more. I hate myself for thinking you could love me as much as I love you."

Jayden stood stock still unable to believe his ears. He could register her tears, the sight of them tearing at his heart; his body felt the swoosh of air and every hard whack of the pillow; he could taste the dryness in his mouth.

But his ears failed him. He couldn't hear anything. Only the hammering of his heart. Was he dreaming? Would he wake up alone in his car and realize he'd made up this moment?

He bit his lip and that felt real enough. But her words...how could he make sense of her words? She loved him? *Him?*

He shook his head. "You fell in love with a lie."

"No, Brown Bear," Nicole said with a sad laugh. "I fell in love with you." She picked up the pillow and put it back on the couch. "Feel free to walk out on me now. You wouldn't be the first. And don't worry, your mother can stay until you find her another place. You may think I'm heartless, but I'm not."

"I know you're not." He held his hands out to the side, helpless. His voice broke when he spoke. "I have nothing to offer you."

She stared at him amazed. "Really?"

Jayden frowned, confused by her expression. "You've given me so much and I haven't given you anything." He placed a hand over his chest. "All I can give you is my heart and that's—"

"You saved my life."

"What?"

"I said you saved my life."

"I helped you at the wedding, you weren't going to die."

"I don't mean that. I mean my entire life. My life hasn't been the same since I met you. It was colorless, ordinary. But you made it brighter. You actually cared about me. I've never had that before. I'm always the one listening to others, but you listened to me. You made me feel special."

"You are special."

"Then why are you throwing me away?"

Jayden waved his hand. "First of all that's impossible. Second of all," he tapped his chest, "only months ago I was working nights in a warehouse. I lied my way into IT consulting. I have to budget every time I got out with you. I—"

"Do you love me?"

He shook his head in frustration. "Of course I love you, but—"

"Are you too proud to stay with me? Do you hate that I make more money than you do?"

He sighed. "No."

"Then let me help you."

He looked away, his gaze falling on his reflection in a glass clock hanging on the wall. He didn't like the man he saw there. "Loving you isn't enough."

She moved closer and turned his face to her. "The funny thing about love is that it can't be measured. You don't know how much it means to hear you say you love me. Helping you makes me happy; it's as simple as that. No exchanges, no transactions just two people who want to be with each other and help each other the best they can."

He hesitated.

"Don't be too proud. Please say yes." She wrapped her arms around his waist and pressed her cheek against his chest. He could feel her trembling. "Say yes to staying with me and growing your business. You can help me manage the property. Take Coco for walks and—"

He slid his arms around her and held her close. He didn't want her to be afraid. "Yes."

She released a happy sigh then stepped back and looked up at him. "Be honest. It was the mention of walking Coco that changed your mind, didn't it?"

He glanced at the dog. "Of course. She's got me wrapped around her little paw. Plus I owe her."

"For what?"

He drew her back into his arms and pressed his lips against her forehead. "Leading you to me."

"I saw your momma's man some place he shouldn't be."

Jayden stared at Francis as he stacked another box inside the storage space. Jayden was helping him move his mother and sister's VeggieLiteDrink boxes into a storage unit. Business wasn't going well. They hadn't chosen the best day to move either. Since it was an outside unit the summer heat bared down on the asphalt and them, soaking their clothes with sweat. Perhaps his friend was suffering the beginnings of heatstroke. He handed him a box then said, "You need to take a break. Let's get something to drink."

"Why? We're almost done."

"You're getting confused."

"About what?"

Jayden wiped sweat from his forehead. "My mum."

"I'm not confused. I did. I saw your momma's man."

"My mum doesn't have a man."

"Yes, she does."

Jayden took off his gloves and rested his fists on his hips. "No, she doesn't."

"Well...then she's real cozy with a second cousin or something because I saw her with a man."

Jayden slapped the gloves hard in his open palm. "Where?"

Francis sent him an uneasy look. "At the mall. In the place where people eat."

"The eatery?"

He nodded. "I saw them together."

"And you said you saw this man again?"

"Yup. And he shouldn't have been there."

"Where did you see this guy?"

Francis lowered his gaze uncomfortable. "Some place I shouldn't have been neither."

Jayden slapped him on the shoulder with his gloves. "Why are you looking down like that? Think I'm going to talk to your PO?" Francis had been in and out of prison and was always complaining about how his parole officer was always up his behind. "You can trust me."

Francis lifted his gaze and shrugged, chagrined. "I know. Doesn't matter, I ain't saying nothing specific. I'm just saying I saw him. Your momma needs to be careful who she hangs with."

Jayden gritted his teeth. He thought she'd learned that lesson before. But it seemed she needed a reminder.

DIONNE GRIPPED the doorframe as she stared into her

son's face. She'd seen that look before. It wasn't good. He'd found out, she didn't know how—she didn't care how—she only knew that her precious secret had been discovered and Jayden wasn't happy about it. She had to be calm. She had to handle this well. She looked down at his sweaty T-shirt. "I know you're upset about something, but you can come back after you've showered."

He forced his way into the cottage and closed the door.

"Mum, who is he?"

She held her cane tight. "What are you talking about?"

"The man you're seeing."

She swallowed. "Jayden, I'm not—"

He briefly closed his eyes as if in pain and held up his hand. "Be careful how you respond," he warned in a low voice. "You promised not to lie to me again."

She sighed. "He's just a friend."

His hand fell to his side. "No, he's not. He's much more than a friend. That's why you didn't tell me about him."

Dionne threw up her hands. "How could I tell you anything when I knew you'd react like this?"

Jayden pounded the wall with his fist. "I don't like finding out you're seeing a man behind my back."

"What are you? My lover? I don't owe you—"

Jayden shook his head and said in a soft voice, "Don't get ugly, Mum. You don't want to do that. Unless he told you—"

"He hasn't forced me to do or say anything. I'm a grown woman with my own mind. Do you think you're the only one who should be happy? You have Nicole. Who am I supposed to have now?"

"Someone who deserves you." Jayden opened the door. "I'm going to take a shower and when I return you're going to tell me everything you know about this man." He stepped out the door then turned to her. "And if you try to deceive and I find out, you'll have a second son you never see again."

OF COURSE HE WAS BLUFFING. He'd never abandon his mother, no matter how angry she made him. And right now if he could punch a hole through two cement blocks he would.

Jayden bent his head and let the hot water of the shower sting his skin as if he'd been attacked by red fire ants. The pain felt good.

He needed pain. Pain kept him from rage.

He'd kept secrets from his mother, but he'd never imagined she'd keep secrets from him. Not again. Why didn't she trust him? Hadn't he proven himself to her?

The look in her eyes hurt. She'd looked at him as if he were her jailer. As if he were keeping her from being free. He appreciated freedom too much to steal it from somebody else. Especially her and yet...

He never said she had to be alone the rest of her life. He only told her to be careful. How could he protect her if she wouldn't let him? What if there were signs she missed again? Signs he missed?

Jayden shook his head, turned off the water and

rested his forehead against the white ceramic tiles. If she only knew how much she hurt him with her words and distrust. There were times he felt he couldn't do enough. That no matter how much he tried, he'd failed her somehow.

He closed his eyes. He wouldn't fail this time. It would be different now. He wouldn't let any man come into his mother's life and isolate her from him. He wouldn't be made the enemy. He wouldn't be too busy to be around her. He'd always take notice. That had been the problem the first time. Jayden had barely interacted with Henry. When his mother married him it had angered and surprised him, but he thought she was being reckless. He never imagined she could be in danger.

He stepped outside of the shower and toweled himself dry. Was the past repeating itself? Back then he'd been so focused on work and a new relationship that he hadn't paid attention either.

He wouldn't make that same mistake this time. He would discover whoever this new man was and he would make his presence known. And if the man wasn't scared off by that, then he'd better treat his mother like a queen or suffer the consequences.

CHAPTER TWENTY-NINE

She'd turned into her father.

Nicole had never thought that would be possible. She knew she had his nose, his charm, but felt confident that she'd escaped his lesser traits.

She'd been wrong.

She was a cheater. Not a fully fledged one, not yet anyway, but close because ever since she'd let Jayden move in with her she'd cheated on him in her mind.

She felt awful about it, but couldn't help herself. She thought about another man and that man wasn't Jayden. He didn't have a name, but he did have a face and a body. A great body. She first noticed him in her neighborhood two weeks ago as she drove to work, she saw him jogging in the opposite direction. He wore red shorts and a fitted blue T-shirt, that clung to a body built for movement. She'd seen the same red shorts and blue T-shirt in Jayden's laundry basket but doubted they'd look that good on him.

The man smiled and waved as if he expected her to stare. Her cheeks burned at being caught and she looked away. She took another route to work the next day.

But she saw him again, briefly, at a Panera Bread. She sat at acorner table that gave her a view of the entrance, waiting for Jayden, when she looked up and saw a devastatingly handsome man come through the front glass doors dressed in dark trousers and a grey shirt. One woman, who was leaving the front counter with her tray, stared at him so long that she crashed into a table. Fortunately, the woman managed not to spill her tray. The man asked if she was okay and she nodded before hurrying to her table.

Then the man did something amazing. He caught her eye, lifted his hand and waved. Her heart lurched and her mouth went dry. He was so beautifully made she couldn't help but be flattered by the attention. Clearly he was new to the neighborhood and saw her as a friendly face. She weakly waved back. She'd have to tell him she was seeing someone else.

But still...awful woman that she was...she, for a moment, only a moment, imagined him coming to her table and sitting down with her. She felt a raw, primal desire to know more about him. He was the kind of man a woman would want to show off. The kind of man she used to be with. Nicole stared down at the gray table and groaned.

Was this her mind's way of rebelling because of Jayden's past? His looks? Did she now think less of him because he depended on her? She thought she was a better woman than that. She told herself that it didn't matter that he wasn't successful, that he wasn't fit. She had someone wonderful. She loved him. She'd told him so and he loved her back. How could she betray him like this?

Had she gotten bored because their relationship had become routine? Because he was no longer a mystery to her? Had she lost interest? She hoped not. Jayden was different than anyone else she'd ever dated. That was a good thing.

Hadn't she learned that successful, good-looking men led to heartache? She closed her eyes and took a deep breath. When she opened her eyes she saw Jayden sitting across from her with a big grin on his face. Her traitorous thoughts returned to normal.

He reached for the garden vegetable soup with pesto and tomato mozzarella flatbread she'd ordered for him. "Mediating?"

"Yes," she managed, rubbing her hands in her lap. "I always get anxious waiting, afraid you won't show up."

He winked. "Then I won't keep you waiting next time."

Nicole sighed happy. He was good enough for her. She didn't need someone to make her heart race the way it used to.

But the terrible daydreams continued. At the strangest moments she saw the other man instead of Jayden. She saw someone bigger, stronger, fitter, sexier. She'd looked at Jayden's back and could only see the other man's wide shoulders.

The next morning, she imagined the man in her

kitchen whipping eggs before she blinked and then saw Jayden's smile again. That's when she realized she was like her father. That she was doomed to ruin something good. But she didn't want to. Her father hurt people. She didn't want to do that. She'd fight to keep her feelings under control. She wouldn't let anything ruin this relationship.

But over the next couple of weeks this phantom man seemed to grow stronger and stronger in her mind.

She knew she was in trouble when he made love to her. She didn't see Jayden at all. She saw this gorgeous stranger and it was intoxicating, thrilling to be in his arms. She couldn't go back. How could she do this to him? How could she be this way? She had to break up with him. Cheating in her mind wasn't fair to him; she wasn't thinking about him if she stayed. He could find someone else. Someone who truly cared about him.

But she didn't want to lose him either. It was stupid to throw her life away because of a fantasy and that reality faced her one hot Saturday afternoon when Jayden entered the house like a mad bear. He'd gone to help his friend move some boxes but the task had taken longer than she'd thought.

"Was it harder than you thought?" she called out to him when she heard the front door slam.

Jayden stood in the doorway. "I need to go take a shower."

She tossed her tablet aside, where she'd been reading the latest edition of *Psychology Today*, and started to stand. "Need help?"

He didn't smile back. Instead he raised his hand and

said, "I'm sorry. I can't talk right now," before he left. Minutes later she heard the shower running.

She waited for him outside the bathroom door. "Can you talk now?" she asked the moment he appeared, freshly showered and smelling like lavender.

He bit his lip and shook his head, looking as sad as a hurt puppy left out in the rain.

She gently touched his arm and he didn't wince or flinch and she knew that meant he trusted her.

It was a hard earned trust she wouldn't throw away. She loved him completely and it was at that moment that the other man disappeared from her thoughts. She'd made her choice and it was this man. She didn't need flashier or sexier. When he hurt she hurt. She took his large hand. "What happened, Brown Bear?"

He lowered his gaze.

She squeezed his hand. "Is it Francis?"

He shook his head.

"You can tell me."

He took a deep steadying breath. "Mum's seeing a man and she was keeping it from me. After all I've done for her...that she can't trust me..." He shook his head. "I don't know."

Nicole stroked his arm, hearing the pain in his voice. "I'm sure it's not that. My mother used to keep men from me all the time."

"Your mum's different."

"I know." Her mother found jerks, but not beaters. "What are you going to do?"

"I can't stop her, but I want to know more. I'm going to talk to her now."

"I think you should calm down first."

"I am calm."

Nicole shook her head. "No, you're not. She's not going anywhere. You can talk to her later. I'll check on her for you. Go and sit down and watch something mindless for awhile or play with Coco. That always cheers me up."

He kissed her on the forehead. "Thank you." Moments later she heard the sound of Coco's paws; the squeak of one of her toys and Jayden saying "good girl."

She left them in the living room to go talk to Dionne who looked a mess when she opened the door to Nicole's knock. Her eyes were red and puffy from crying.

"I'm sorry. I didn't mean to pull you into this," she said.

Nicole stepped inside and closed the door. "I care about your son and I care about you. There's nothing to apologize about." She waited, but when Dionne didn't immediately say or do anything else she said, "May I sit down?"

"Of course. Yes, please. Would you like some tea?"

Nicole took a seat, trying her best not to remember the last time she'd been there and gotten burned. "No, thank you. I only stopped by to check that you're okay."

Dionne took a seat in front of her, her hands pressed between her knees. "He's so angry with me right now."

"He's hurt more than angry."

"You didn't see his face. I know my son."

Nicole paused surprised by Dionne's words. She didn't know her son as well as she thought if she only believed he was angry at her for keeping a secret from him. But it wasn't her place to judge. Nicole had never seen his rage before and he had nearly killed a man. That was something Dionne knew and maybe feared.

"Are you protecting this man? Do you think Jayden will hurt him like—?" She stopped when Dionne's eyes widened like saucers.

"No," she said in a rush. "Oh no. I'm not afraid of that."

"But you're afraid of something."

She placed her hands on her lap, hung her head and whispered something.

Nicole leaned closer. "I'm sorry?"

"I'm afraid of being alone."

"But you're not alone. You have friends and your son loves you."

"I could lose him." Her hands trembled in her lap. "I could lose everything."

Nicole stared at her helpless, thinking of the fragile cocoon again. Dionne was a woman filled with fear and she didn't want to make it worse. "You're not going to lose him. Right now he's...processing this. I know in time he'll be able to accept whoever this man is."

"He's a good man." She looked up with the ghost of a smile. "You'd like him. Ernestina introduced me to him."

"She...did...what?" Nicole's voice grew soft.

Dionne covered her mouth like a frightened child. "Oh no. I wasn't supposed to say anything. Please don't—"

Nicole plastered on a smile and stood. If she didn't leave soon she was going to lose her temper. *Ernestina!*

"It's okay. I'm glad my mother could help you. Now I'd better go back and check on Jayden."

She slammed the door the moment she entered the house. Jayden rushed to her with Coco close behind.

"Mum upset you?"

"No," Nicole said between clenched teeth. "Your mother's a doll. It's my mother who—" She stopped. Took a deep breath and counted to ten before she said, "My mother introduced them." She waved his unspoken questions away. "I'll deal with her later. Right now I think you should meet this new man on neutral ground."

THE COFFEE SHOP seemed like safe territory. Nicole had been able to convince Dionne to meet there. She hadn't spoken to her mother yet—that would come later—first she wanted to heal the wound between mother and son.

She was the first one to arrive. Dionne planned to arrive with her new man and Jayden said he had a quick errand to run then would come later. Nicole scanned the area to see where would be the perfect place to sit then saw someone who made her know the day wasn't going to go well.

CHAPTER THIRTY

Across the room near the front counter, she saw the jerk who'd keyed her car. He had a smirk on his face. She wondered why then realized she didn't care. He wasn't her problem. If he wanted to say something, he'd have to come over to her. She wouldn't make that easy.

She lowered her gaze and turned around to find a table as far from him as possible when a pair of red high heel shoes came into view. She lifted her gaze and stared into the eyes of a viper. An attractive black woman with lipstick as red as her shoes.

"You messed with my man and my car," she said.

Nicole inwardly sighed. Now she understood why the jerk had looked so smug. He was going to let his woman fight his battle for him. "I apologize for one not the other."

The woman narrowed her eyes. She took a step forward and used her spiked heel to crush one of Nicole's toes, which wasn't hard since she was wearing open-toed sandals. "Are you disrespecting my car?"

It happened so fast Nicole didn't have a chance to react. Her foot felt like it was on fire. She dug her nails into the side of the woman's neck. "No, I'm disrespecting your man. A woman like you can find better."

The woman stepped back and touched her neck then checked her hand for blood. "I don't know what game you're playing."

"No game. But I will charge you with assault if you don't get out of my way."

The woman leaned forward and said in a low, threatening voice, "You want to make me?"

Nicole boldly held her gaze, even though her foot throbbed and standing hurt. "If I have to, I will." The woman began to move away. "I will go so wild they'll cart us both off to jail." The woman took a step back. "If you think I damaged your car, how would you like to see what I'd do to your face?"

Nicole saw the woman's eyes widen in fear and she quickly retreated. She smiled in triumph. "That's what I thought." She turned to look back at the jerk, but a man's broad chest blocked her view. And the brown shirt looked familiar. She looked up and saw the handsome phantom man. She'd thought she'd scared the woman off but his large presence had.

"Causing trouble?" Jayden said.

Nicole opened her mouth to respond then stopped. Wait. Why did this man sound like Jayden? And why was he wearing Jayden's shirt? Nicole felt faint as the pieces came together.

There was no other man. It had been Jayden all along. He was the new man she'd seen jogging, in her kitchen, in her bed. He'd changed and she hadn't even realized it.

Why hadn't she noticed that he'd lost weight and gotten more toned; that as his business grew so did his confidence; the way he walked and carried himself? She hadn't cheated on him even in her thoughts. She'd fallen in love with him all over again.

She felt her knees grow weak. Jayden caught her before she hit the ground. "What's wrong?" he said alarmed.

"I need to sit down." With her hand on his arm, she limped to a chair and collapsed. "I'm so glad you're—" She stopped when he suddenly swore and fell on his knees in front of her. He gingerly took off her shoe before he looked up at her and said, "What happened?"

She looked down at her swollen toe. In the shock of fully seeing the new Jayden, she'd forgotten the jerk and his woman. "I think she broke my toe. They're probably long gone since you scared her off," Nicole said when Jayden turned his head searching for the pair.

"This is bad," he said in a grim voice. "We should take you to—"

"No, not the hospital again." The nurse there already thought she was in a bad situation this would only confirm his suspicions. "I can heal this at home."

Jayden took out his phone. "We'll have to postpone our meeting," he told her then said on the phone, "Hi, Mum. No, it's okay. I'm not calling because of...You're not that late. Mum, it doesn't matter..." He sighed. "I look forward to meeting him too, but we're going to have to cancel. No, I haven't changed my mind. No, Mum I need you to listen...I know it's important I... Something's come up and I have to take Nicole home. No, it's not serious. I'll explain later." He put his phone away then reached for her.

Nicole leaned back. "What are you doing?"

"I'm going to carry you to my car."

"I can walk there."

"That will make it worse."

"I can hop then." She stood up on one foot. "Don't embarrass me."

He sniffed. "You'd prefer to hop out of here like a rabbit instead of letting me carry you like a princess?"

"You can treat me like a princess later. Now help me to the door."

"You are one stubborn woman," he said, letting her lean heavily against him. "I'll drive you home then come back for your car."

"Thank you. Sorry about this. This was to be an important day."

Jayden sighed. "I thought I'd gotten you out of that habit." He held the door open for her. "This wasn't your fault."

Nicole shook her head with a touch of chagrin. "Somehow I knew I had this coming."

CHAPTER THIRTY-ONE

What she didn't expect was an ambush at work.

The witches were waiting for her when she hobbled into the office. It had been five days since the coffee shop incident and she walked on crutches, she'd kept from an accident years ago. On Monday when she'd come into work with them, they'd asked about her bandaged foot and she'd told them a story about being distracted and dropping an iron on her foot then gone about her day. She thought her lie was good until that Friday afternoon when they called her into the group therapy room at the end of the day.

They all sat in front of her with composed expression, although instead of the usual self-satisfied grin on Kelvin's face there was the hint of worry.

Kelvin never worried.

"We really think it's important that you know you can trust us," Yasmine said, using a voice she typically reserved for clients.

"We're here for you," Carla added, her tone just as modulated.

"But we think that you should take some time off while you deal with personal issues," Kelvin said getting right to the point.

"We have decided that we will take over your patient load in your absence," Carla said.

Nicole stared at them stunned. "What personal issues? What absence? I'm not going anywhere."

"Maybe you should," Yasmine said.

Carla nodded. "We have been worried about you. The bruises, the lies."

Nicole blinked confused. "What bruises? What lies?"

Kelvin pointed at her face. "Your eye, for one."

Carla crossed her legs. "That you tried to cover up with makeup."

He pointed lower. "Your arm."

"That you tried to disguise by wearing long sleeves."

He motioned to her leg. "And your foot."

"They were all accidents," Nicole said.

"You really want us to believe that you dropped an iron on your foot?"

"Okay, so that was a lie. The truth was more embarrassing. I got into an...altercation with a woman because I insulted her boyfriend and smashed the side mirror on her car, which I didn't know was her car at the time, so she stomped on my foot."

They nodded.

"And the arm?" Yasmine asked.

"I was with a friend and she accidentally spilled hot tea on me."

They all nodded again.

"And the black eye was also an accident?" Yasmine said.

Nicole sighed. "Yes, I was at my mother's wedding about to catch the bouquet when someone elbowed me and I fell to the ground. It was crazy."

They nodded.

"I'm telling the truth." She reached for her phone. "I can get someone to show you the footage if you want."

Yasmine waved her effort away. "There's no need."

"Because we know that's not the full truth," Carla said.

"But I have proof that—"

Carla pressed her hands together. "We know you're dating a violent criminal."

Nicole dropped her phone on the carpet and stared at them shocked. "What?"

"We're not here to judge you. Even intelligent woman like you—"

Nicole's brows shot up. "Intelligent as opposed to stupid?"

"Can find themselves in abusive relationships," Carla continued.

Nicole snatched her phone off the ground and shoved it back into her handbag. "This is ridiculous. I understand, and appreciate your concern, but I'm *not* in an abusive relationship and I'm definitely not dating a dangerous criminal."

Yasmine nodded, sad. "It's perfectly normal to be in denial about this and lie to protect—"

Nicole's voice cracked with frustration. "I'm not in

denial and I'm not lying. I swear. And for the last time I'm not—"

"We know you're seeing a man who served time in prison for attempted murder," Carla said. "I know this because I saw him drop you off. His name is Jayden Cassell."

Nicole rubbed her forehead, an icy fear twisting her heart. They were reading the situation all wrong. She took a deep breath and let her hand fall to her lap. "I know who he is. So I know his real name and I know about his past. In a moment of anger he did something he regretted but he was protecting someone else. I know he'd never hurt me."

"Did you know he's also my brother-in-law?"

Jayden Cassell. Carla Cassell. She remembered making that connection before, but Jayden had told her he didn't have any sisters. However, she'd never made the connection that Carla might be married to his brother.

"He's never met me," Carla continued as if to answer Nicole's silent question. "But I've seen pictures of him."

"And he isn't the image that we think should be associated with you...or us," Yasmine said.

Kelvin nodded. "Think about our reputation."

Nicole glanced up at the ceiling unable to know how to respond. One moment she's an abused woman, the next moment she was dating a violent criminal and now she was a liability to their practice. "My private life has never affected the business. I've always been a consummate professional. My patients trust me." And she was making excellent progress with them. Only last week she'd finally gotten Ben and Amelia Horowitz to use the words "we" and "us" instead of "I" and "me." It was the first time she had hope for them. Her relationship with Jayden had made her more empathetic; a better counselor. And she wanted to help even more than she had in the past. How could they try to take that away from her now? "I have never—"

Kelvin adjusted his watch and cleared his throat. His brown eyes still held a hint of concern, but it was also mixed with determination. "We don't want to have to remind you of the contractual agreement you signed. But if we have to, we will."

They were giving her an option that wasn't really one. They wanted her gone.

"Well, you always did want the Queen Suite," Nicole said without humor.

"Your office will still be here when you come back," he said.

Not "if" but "when." So they did expect her to return, that was good, but she sensed a catch. She folded her arms. "What do you want?"

"We want you to take time off to think about whether continuing this relationship is worth it," Yasmine said.

Carla leaned forward. "And if you need a route of escape—"

Nicole gripped her hands into fists. "I'm not in an abusive relationship."

"We're only a phone call away if you need us," Carla said as if Nicole hadn't spoken.

~

SHE DIDN'T CRY.

She wanted to but she held back her tears as she gathered some useless items from her desk. She didn't dare call Jayden to come pick her up. Instead she called for a ride.

She didn't cry in the backseat of the blue Cadillac either.

Although she really wanted to. She swallowed hard when the driver asked about her bandaged foot and she lied smoothly and listened to the driver share about the time she'd broken her leg while rock climbing.

The tears threatened to fall down her face when the driver stopped in front of her house. But she still didn't cry. She thanked the driver and stepped out of the car.

But the moment she turned and saw Jayden's surprised expression as he rushed towards her, hot tears rolled down her face and she collapsed in the driveway.

CHAPTER THIRTY-TWO

Agony.

His angel was in agony and he didn't know why. Jayden cupped Nicole's tear soaked face, his eyes searching her face while Coco licked her hand. "Where do you hurt? Let me—"

Nicole shook her head and said in a small voice, "Please help me."

Helplessness gripped him. He didn't know what she needed or how he could help her. He lifted her up, carried her inside then placed her on the couch. When he moved to leave her, she grabbed his arm. "Please don't leave me."

Why was she begging him as if she expected him to refuse her? "I'm getting your crutches and handbag from the driveway. I'll be right back." He quickly gathered her things and put them in the closet then returned to the living room where he found Nicole curled up into a ball.

He knelt in front of her afraid to touch her. "Honey?"

She squeezed her eyes shut, tears leaking from under her lids. "It hurts so much."

"Where?" he asked, his anxiety building. "I can't help you if you don't tell me where."

She took a deep breath before she sat up. She wiped her eyes and fixed her features into a mask of calm. "I shouldn't have said that. I'm sorry. I don't mean to scare you."

She scared him even more when she started to apologize. "What happened?"

She lowered her head, her voice broke in misery. "I can't tell you. Not yet. Not without crying."

He looked up at her, his eyes pleading, his heart racing. "What can I do?"

"Just hold me." She shook her head when he started to speak. "Please Brown Bear. No questions. Just hold me."

Jayden growled low in his throat before he sat down beside her and pulled her into his arms, holding her close.

Nicole settled into his embrace feeling safe in his arms.

Safe. She hadn't always felt that way.

She didn't feel that way with the shadow man. The one who came into her dreams and turned them into nightmares she couldn't remember.

But she remembered them now. The shadow man liked to come into her room. Sometimes at night, but mostly in the afternoon when she returned home from school.

For the first time she saw the shadow man's face: Her mother's second husband. The one who was always home because he couldn't work anymore. The one who always liked to come home with treats. The one her mother and sister adored.

She didn't like him. She said he was a bad man. But no one believed her. They thought she was lying.

"Why would he do that to your bicycle?" her mother chided her on the way home from the hospital. Nicole had broken her arm when the shadow man had stuck a rod in her bicycle wheel, causing her to fly forward and break her arm. "You can get clumsy."

She wasn't lying. But no one believed her.

And it hurt. It hurt that her house wasn't safe. It hurt that her mother thought she was a liar. It hurt that her sister was too young to understand.

It hurt so much that when Aunt Cleo came to visit she cried and told her everything, not caring if she thought she was a liar too. She told her how he'd tricked her. How he'd come into her bedroom and told her he had a sweet ice lolly for her. He said it was his special ice lolly and he wanted her to suck it.

But it wasn't sweet and she didn't like it. He tried to force her so she bit him. That's why he'd made her fall off her bike. She also told her about the other woman who came to visit and how he played with her.

And then she stared at her aunt with red, raw eyes waiting for Aunt Cleo to call her a liar too.

But her aunt believed her. She never saw the shadow man again.

And when he went away her mother didn't speak to her for awhile. She blamed Nicole for ruining her marriage, for shaming her in front of her sister.

So Nicole started to hate Aunt Cleo because it was easier than hating her mother. The one she had to live with, the one who'd given her life. The one who preferred being with a man rather than her children.

That's when Nicole's guilt settled into her heart. She felt guilty for being alive, for being the cause of her mother's pain, and started apologizing.

If her mother hadn't had two daughters to look after on her own, she would be free and happy. It was her fault her mother was lonely. She apologized to every man in her mother's life, hoping they'd like her. She'd cried at her mother's third wedding because she didn't want to live with a man again. The memory of the shadow man had been pushed to the back of her mind as a faint thought, but the fear still lingered.

But there was nothing to be afraid of. Aunt Cleo said so at the rehearsal dinner; Nicole pretended not to hear her. But her aunt had been right. It never happened again.

Now she felt like a helpless child again.

How could she get anyone to believe her? She wasn't dating a monster. She wasn't lying.

"Brown Bear," Nicole said her voice barely above a whisper.

"Hmm."

"I have to tell you something," she said before she

shared her painful past. And as she spoke Jayden was reminded of his turtle Lucy finally peeking her soft, tender head out of her hard shell, trusting him.

When Nicole finished her story, he understood and wanted to protect her even more. He caressed her cheek and said in a gentle voice, "What happened today?"

"I was asked to leave."

"Why?"

"It's partly my fault. If I hadn't lied about the iron falling on my foot maybe—"

"Tell me."

She drew away from him and met his gaze. "It's a misunderstanding. They're making assumptions because of my accidents."

Jayden frowned confused. "Your accidents? What about them?"

"They don't think they are accidents. They think they were deliberate." She paused. "That they're because of you."

CHAPTER THIRTY-THREE

Color left his face.

"I explained everything," Nicole said taking his hand in hers. It felt strangely cold. "But they won't listen. And then...Carla mentioned your past and that made it worse. They're threatening to force me out unless I... There's a special provision in our contract that states certain 'personal circumstances' can lead to our dismissal from the practice."

"Who's Carla?"

Nicole paused. She'd hoped he wouldn't ask that. "One of my colleagues."

"But you said her name in a special way. As if it were important."

"She's you're sister-in-law."

Jayden bit his lip and slowly nodded. "So you could lose your job because of me." He sat back with an eerie calm. "I can't blame them. A man with my past would be suspicious."

"I'm going to take a week, let my foot heal more and then I'm going to talk to them."

"I was going to tell you this later, but...my business has improved enough so I can move out."

"You don't have to do that."

"I do. Not only because of this but because I need to get Mum away from here. Until I have a chance to find out more about the man she's seeing, I don't want him to know where she lives or where you live either."

"I'm sure he's not—"

"I'm not sure of anything. But Francis told me he saw this man where he shouldn't be and Francis doesn't lie. He also knows every trap house around here."

Nicole frowned. "Trap house?"

"A drug house. If Mum is mixed up with a man like that I have to get her away from here. It's the best way to keep you both safe."

"It may be too late. He could already know where she lives."

"Then I need to move her sooner than I thought."

Nicole tightened her grip on his hand. "I scared you away, didn't I? Because I told you about my past you think—"

He shook his head. "It's not that."

"Please don't leave me. The thought of losing you hurts so much. Please Brown Bear. Stay with me."

Jayden sighed and gathered her in his arms again. He carried her to the bedroom where they made love and he whispered her name over and over again; she held him as tight as she could before she fell asleep in his embrace.

But when she woke up the next morning, he was gone.

CHAPTER THIRTY-FOUR

"What's wrong with you?" Brian asked his wife as they sat together in the den that evening. She hadn't been able to sit still and kept sighing through the action movie on the flat screen. "Are you bored or something?"

Carla put the movie on pause just as a red mustang was flying through the air. She turned to her husband, glad he smelled like candy apples. That meant he was in a good mood. "I don't know if I did the right thing."

"About what?"

She sighed.

He frowned. "Stop doing that."

"I think I know why your mother has been calling you, or rather me, so much recently."

"Why?"

"Jayden's hurting his girlfriend."

Brian's voice turned cold. "Someone's been lying. What did she say?"

"She didn't say anything. I made a guess and then I saw the evidence."

"What evidence?"

"Of the abuse. Her name's Nicole. Nicole Harrison. You know, the woman I work with. She can be a hardass but she's good. Anyway, several months ago she came into work with a black eye and then a bandaged arm—"

Brian studied her. "And she blamed him?"

"No, she defended him. She said we had it all wrong, but abused woman lie all the time."

"She's not lying." Brian turned back to the flat screen and continued watching the movie.

Carla put it on pause again. "You know some men go into prison and come out worse than when they went in."

"That's not Jayden."

"You don't know your brother anymore."

"I know him," Brian said his tone challenging her to contradict him. "I may not have seen him in years, but I *know* him. And from the stories I've told you about him, you know him too. So what are you hiding from me?"

Carla sighed and lowered her head. Brian knew her too well. "It's been almost a week and...I feel guilty. I keep seeing Nicole's face. She looked so horrified and shocked when we told her to leave him."

"What did you do?"

She rubbed her hands together. "It seemed like a good idea at the time, but I may have done something I should have talked to you about first."

"Like?"

She nervously licked her lower lip. "But I didn't think much of it until your mother called me two days ago. This time I answered my phone because I wanted to make sure she was okay and she said she wasn't because Jayden wouldn't eat anything. He only works and sleeps and she thinks it's because she's seeing someone and had kept it from him."

Brian surged to his feet. "Mum's seeing someone?"

"Yes. Jayden hasn't met him yet but she said he's acting strange. He broke up with his girlfriend and forced them to move—"

Brian powered off the movie. "Where is he staying?"

"I didn't ask. Where are you going?" she asked when he turned and walked into the hall.

Brian headed for the door. "I'm going to save my brother, but first I need you to do me a favor..."

CHAPTER THIRTY-FIVE

Somehow she'd expected there to be two of them. When Jayden mentioned he had a brother, Nicole imagined a man as big as him, not the tall, refined stranger on her doorstep who introduced himself as Brian Cassell. He was the complete opposite. He had handsome looks made for the camera.

"Thank you for agreeing to see me," he said.

"Carla said it was urgent."

"It is." He glanced down at her bandaged foot. "Answer me honestly. Did a man do that? And if a man did do that, was that man my brother?"

"No. A man did not do this. Your brother has never hurt me."

He nodded satisfied. "That's what I thought."

"Your wife doesn't think so."

He let out a breath. "She's already feeling guilty. She's always been a little jealous of you. She keeps mentioning wanting to be in the Queen Suite. I think she saw an opportunity to get inside. Not that that's the only reason. I think she wanted to believe the story she told the others."

Nicole folded her arms. "Have you come here to apologize on her behalf?"

"No, I need your help."

"My help?"

He nodded. "If you can manage..." His words trailed off and he looked at her foot again.

"It's much better now," Nicole said quickly. "I can walk. What do you need?"

"I need you to come with me. We need to do a little rescue."

"Rescue?"

"It's about time my brother stops sacrificing himself for my mum."

He ached all over.

Jayden lay stretched out on the couch and flipped through channels but his body felt like it was on fire. He craved Nicole's touch so much it hurt. He couldn't sleep at night. He'd grown so used to her lying beside him that it felt alien without her. Damn. He even missed Coco and her soft fur and little wet tongue.

He'd survive the separation of course. It was what he had to do. His mother had told him the name of her new man and after a quick online search he'd come up clean. But Jayden knew he'd have to dig deeper. It wasn't easy to find out if a man frequented trap houses through a search engine.

At least he'd found them both a place. Thanks to Nicole's help establishing Cassell Consulting as a corporation, he was able to rent the apartment through his company. It came completely furnished and had a great view. The place also had a swimming center and business suite he could rent, if he needed, to meet with clients. He'd gone up in the world. He could afford a nice dinner at a fine restaurant in a restructured mansion like the one Nicole had taken him on their first date, without breaking into a sweat. He could buy clothes, jewelry if he wanted to.

But he couldn't share any of it with the woman he loved.

He scowled at the clock when someone rang the doorbell. It was late. "Who is it?"

"It's me."

Jayden sat up. The voice sounded strangely like his brother. "Who is me?"

"Open the damn door," Brian said.

Jayden quickly surveyed the room to make sure it looked decent. What was his brother doing there? How had he found him? He took a deep breath and opened the door. He blinked when he saw Brian. He hadn't seen him in years. "What are you..." His voice fell away and he stopped breathing when he saw Nicole. His heart squeezed in anguish. "You shouldn't be here," he said his voice raw.

Brian blocked his view of her and said, "Is Mum here?"

He swallowed, his throat tight, as he struggled to compose himself. "S-she's sleeping."

"Wake her."

"But—"

"Wake her. We have a few things to discuss."

The moment Dionne came into the room and saw Brian sitting on the couch next to Nicole she burst into tears. Jayden gently led her to a seat.

Brian remained unmoved. "Mum, do you know why I'm here?" he asked her.

She shook her head, wiping tears away. "No."

"I'm here because you called and told Carla, Jayden wasn't acting right."

Jayden recovered from his shock of seeing both Brian and Nicole again and looked at his mother stunned. "You did what?"

"I was worried about you," she said.

Brian nodded. "I'm glad to finally hear that. I wish you'd said that years ago when you sent your son to prison for a crime he didn't commit."

CHAPTER THIRTY-SIX

Jayden stood and pointed to the door, his voice filled with anger. "Get out."

Brian ignored him. He turned to Nicole and flashed a brilliant white smile as if he expected a camera flash. "I don't know if you've seen my show "Georgia Secrets" but you could say I was inspired to pitch the idea due to these two." He absently motioned to Dionne and Jayden.

Jayden's voice hardened. "Nicole, you should leave."

Brian rested a hand on her arm. The touch was light, but she could feel the strength of his grip. He didn't plan to let her go anywhere. Not that she felt she could. The sight of seeing Jayden again, desperate to see any hint that he missed her as much as she'd missed him, kept her still. She'd wanted to see signs that he was suffering, even a little, without her. But he wasn't. His new apartment was stylishly furnished and he looked as good as she remembered.

She searched his face, but couldn't read his expression—it was guarded, but it had been guarded before—and he kept his distance from her, as if they were strangers, which hurt even more. "No, Nicole," Brian said, "please stay and hear how this sweet little woman sitting so quiet over there got away with nearly killing a man."

Jayden made a move towards him. "Get out."

Brian turned to him, his eyes dark. "It's okay for you and Mum to live the consequences of your lies. But now Nicole is involved too. Have you thought about that? No, because all you think about it her." He glared at Dionne.

Jayden shook his head. He allowed a brief glance at Nicole and for a moment she saw fear and longing in his gaze before he looked away. "It's not that simple."

"It's very simple," Brian said. "That's why I'm explaining it and you're not." He gestured to a chair. Jayden met his brother's gaze and for what seemed like hours, they glared at each other, the tension in the air sizzling. Finally Brian broke his gaze and sent a significant looked at Nicole. Jayden hesitated then with reluctance, slowly sat down. Brian turned his attention back to Nicole.

"It's amazing the damage a woman can do with an iron skillet. Yes, that night she had a busted lip and a black eye. I couldn't blame her for not being able to take it anymore. She caught him by surprise while he was eating red beans and rice. One whack on the back of the head and he was on the ground. Then she just kept at it. But when her son arrived after a frantic phone call from her, she'd found the perfect fall guy."

"Mummy was sick," Dionne said. "I had to take care of her."

Brian kept his gaze on Nicole. "The way she speaks you'd think she was an only child. She's got two sisters and a brother you know."

Dionne pressed her hands together. "They—"

"Fortunately for her, she had a husband who couldn't remember what had happened and she had a son. A son willing to do anything for her. She sacrificed his youth, his dreams, and his hopes so that she could be free."

Jayden shook his head in annoyance. "Nicole, that's not how it happened. I—"

"He's right," Brian interrupted. "I left out how he punched Mum's husband a couple times to bruise his fists and cover some of the damage she'd already done. I left out how two of the cops were suspicious of the story, something to do with a timestamp on a receipt from a retail store, putting Jayden in another location when neighbors said they heard shouting, but somehow they were convinced to look the other way by their superiors."

"I don't care," Jayden said. "If I had protected her as I should have, it wouldn't have happened."

"She could have come to us. She didn't have to stay."

"When you're in an abusive relationship it's hard to get out."

"I know. That's why I'm trying to get you out of one."

Jayden surged out of his chair, grabbed his brother by the collar and lifted him out of the seat. "That's enough." He dragged him towards the door then released him. "Get out."

Brian stumbled against the wall, smoothed out his

shirt and said with a sad smile, "That's right. Choose her over me again."

Jayden stared at him confused. "What are you talking about?"

Brian folded his arms. "I'm talking about us. You keep talking about protecting her." His voice rose with anger. "But why didn't she think to protect *you*? Is that what a mother does?" He looked past Jayden and stared at Dionne. "Lie to her children and then let them pay for her crime?" He took a step towards her, but Jayden blocked him with his arm. Brian turned to him and softened his voice but years of pain echoed there. "Is that love? She was always looking out for others. When did she look out for *us*?"

"It's not—"

"He's right," Dionne said. "Staying silent in that courtroom was one of the most cowardly things I've ever done in my life. But I was afraid."

"Of what?" Brian demanded.

"Everything. I wanted Jayden to take care of everything. It was what I was used to. My family looked after me, your dear father did the same. He took care of everything. After such an awful experience for so many years I wanted someone to look after me again. It was childish and it wasn't right, but it was how I felt. I've tried to atone. If you read any of my letters you'd know how happy your grandmother was with me. My sister said so. And—"

Brian hung his head in disappointment. "You're doing it again, Mum. Painting a sweet little story and leaving out key details." He flashed Nicole a cold smile.

"I learned how to do that from her." He faced his mother again. "You promised not to hide things from us again, but you're seeing a man and didn't tell us."

"That's my fault," Nicole said.

"None of this is your fault," Jayden said in a sharp tone. But she knew his words weren't said in anger. He was trying to protect her.

"Ernestina introduced them," Nicole said meeting his gaze, hoping he'd understand that he didn't need to protect her. That she was strong enough to face anything. "She can be very persuasive."

"He's a good man," Dionne said.

"Then he'll have no problem meeting with us and answering a few questions," Jayden said.

"Don't scare him away."

"If he's easily scared that's too bad."

"How did you meet him?" Brian asked.

Dionne tapped her mouth. "I already said more than I should have."

"So why stop now?" Brian said.

"Ernestina's been good to me. I don't want to get her into trouble."

"You won't lose her as a friend," Nicole said, sensing Dionne's true fear.

"I met him at the book club. He'll be there this week too."

"Good," Jayden said. "Sounds like a good chance to meet him."

Brian glanced at the clock. "And it's late so I'd better go."

Dionne rushed up to him, her cane pounding on the

ground, and grabbed his arm like a desperate woman. "Forgive me." She fell to her knees. "Please forgive me."

"Mum, get up."

She lowered her head. "I was wrong. I'm sorry. So very sorry."

Brian stood still for a moment then slowly knelt in front of her, tears shining in his eyes. "Thank you." He took a deep breath. "I forgive you." He pointed at Jayden. "Now turn to your firstborn and say the same things."

Jayden reached to lift her up. "She doesn't have to."

"Yes, I do," Dionne said, searching his face. "I'm sorry. I'm sorry I've made you suffer so much."

He nodded. "I know." He kissed her tenderly on the forehead. "You look tired. Go to bed."

She sent a look at Brian and he nodded in agreement. "Goodnight Mum." He paused before he said, "I'll talk to you later," something he hadn't said in years.

Dionne nodded then disappeared into her room.

Once the door was closed, Jayden said, "You shouldn't have come here," but although he looked at Brian, his words were for Nicole. "It doesn't change anything. To the world I'm still a criminal and I don't plan to tell them different."

"At least she now knows the truth." Brian looked at Nicole. "His former fiancée, Monica, actually thought he was guilty even though he told her what he was doing. He won't admit it, but that's what destroyed him the most. That she thought he was capable of killing a man."

"I am capable," Jayden said.

"We all are. But we also need people in our lives who believe us when we say we didn't do something." He folded his arms. "But first we need to find out who this Ernestina woman is and find a way to join her book club."

"You don't have to do that," Nicole said. "She's my mother and I know where and when her next meeting will be."

Brian grinned and rubbed his hands together, eager. "Excellent, we'll all go together. Do I have to bring anything?"

CHAPTER THIRTY-SEVEN

I t took Nicole two seconds to realize her mother wasn't hosting a book club. When Prentice had opened the door and said, "Is your mother expecting you?" Nicole knew something was up. But when she walked into the living room with Brian and Jayden behind her she couldn't believe her eyes.

There were about eight stylish older women and twenty older men in different stages of—interaction. One woman had five men surrounding her; another sat chatting intimately with two. To give them credit they all carried books. Each of a different subject.

"Nicole!" Ernestina said with delight when she saw her daughter. She was dressed in a stylish black blazer, gold blouse and dark trousers. She flashed a bright realtor's smile as if they were prospective house buyers and she was eager for a sale. "You should have told me you were coming." Her gaze shifted to the two men behind her daughter and sharpened with interest. "And you brought guests with you."

"What are you doing?" Nicole said in a low voice.

She gestured to the room and guests with pride. "Hosting a book club."

"Usually, a book club discusses the *same* book at once."

"This is *much* more fun." She pulled a face. "You don't think people *really* get together and discuss books, do you? Especially vibrant women of a certain age. We have so much life to live and I'm helping my friends find the same happiness I did." Before Nicole could reply, she pointed at Jayden and Brian. "I don't believe we've met."

"You've met," Nicole said. "The only reason they're here is to meet the man you introduced to Mrs. Cassell."

Ernestina frowned, confused. "Mrs. Cassell?"

"Dionne," Brian said to clarify. "We're her sons."

Ernestina winked. "Lucky woman. Where is your mother by the way?"

"She couldn't make it tonight."

"Pity, he'll be so disappointed."

Nicole sighed in frustration. "Mom, where is he?"

Ernestina turned and searched the room. "Yes, Randolph Williams." She lowered her voice and said, "He's a plantain. I—"

"I don't care. Just point to him."

She motioned to a suave looking, salt and pepper haired man sitting alone near the window. "He's over there. I put him there on purpose to keep the other women away."

Nicole cast another glance around the room. "I think all the women are well-occupied right now."

Ernestina looked at the woman surrounded by five men. "Giselle can get greedy. And Louelle hasn't arrived yet and can get clingy."

"I don't believe this," Nicole muttered, disgusted.

"Thank you," Jayden said, eager to avert an argument between mother and daughter. "We appreciate this Mrs. Har- Brow- Uh..." He hesitated embarrassed. He'd forgotten which surname to use.

"Just call me Ernestina," she said with a smile.

"If you'll excuse us," Brian said before he and Jayden made their way over to Randolph.

CHAPTER THIRTY-EIGHT

The older man jumped up in fear when he saw them, his eyes wide as if they were gangsters coming to collect. The copy of *Treasure Island* that had been on his lap toppled to the floor.

"Please sit," Brian said in a friendly voice, hoping to put the man at ease. "I'm Brian Cassell and this is my brother Jayden. He only looks mean, but he's usually harmless."

"You look nervous, Williams," Jayden said, taking a seat in front of him. "Do you have something to be nervous about?"

"What my brother is trying to say, is we're interested in getting to know you better since you're dating our mother. Is that okay with you?"

Randolph slowly sat down and nodded.

"What do you do for a living?" Brian asked.

"What were you doing at a drug house?" Jayden asked at the same time. When his brother looked at him shocked, he shrugged and said, "No point beating about the bush."

Randolph cleared his throat, but didn't reply.

"You're not going to deny it?" Jayden pressed.

"No." He hesitated. "It's not something I like to talk about."

"If you want to continue to see our mother you'll start."

"We don't want to see our mother hurt," Brian added.

Randolph lowered his gaze and sighed. "I understand." He picked up the fallen book and placed it on his lap. "I have a granddaughter." He ran his hand over the cover, then along the spine. "I try to check on her every once in a while. Just to see that she's got something to eat...that she's still alive..." He lifted his gaze. "That's why I was there."

Jayden leaned back in his chair and softly swore.

Brian leaned forward and said, "I'm sorry."

Randolph flashed a sad smile. "Thank you. I didn't want to tell your mother and burden her with my problem."

"I doubt she'd see it as a burden." He sent Jayden a private look. "You'll find out she has some family drama of her own."

"She's a wonderful woman. I really care about her. To answer your first question. I'm a retired ophthalmologist."

Brian held out his hand. "A pleasure to meet you."

Randolph shook his hand. "Same." He turned to Jayden, but Jayden only nodded at his outstretched hand.

"Don't worry about him," Brian said. "It takes him awhile to warm up to people."

"I understand."

"I hope you do," Jayden said, his soft voice laced with warning.

Randolph gripped the book in his lap.

"Mum couldn't make it," Brian said. "But if you want to call, I'm sure she'd be happy to hear from you."

"Thanks." He hurried out of the room.

Brian turned to his brother. "You didn't have to scare him."

"Yes, I did."

Brian clasped his hands together. "Well, our work here is almost done."

Jayden frowned. "Almost?"

"Why do you think I suggested we all take the same car?"

Brian nodded to Nicole who was having a heated discussion with her mother. "You have a beautiful woman to comfort. You hardly spoke to her on the way here."

"I told you this doesn't change anything." Jayden watched Nicole wave her finger at her mother before she stormed out of the room. "She's dealing with enough." He looked back at his brother. "My past can hurt her. She could lose her job because of me."

"She won't. I plan to talk to Carla and make sure of that. But even if she did, she'd find another one."

"But Mum—"

"She's not in danger anymore." Brian sighed. "The

truth is you're not trying to protect her. You're trying to protect yourself."

Jayden stiffened. "That's not true. She—"

"You're afraid."

"I'm not afraid."

"Lucy," Brian said in a soft voice, saying the name of Jayden's beloved pet turtle. "Dad."

Jayden looked away.

"Losing something you love hurts, but you don't stop loving because you're afraid of losing it."

Jayden stroked his beard, but continued to avoid his brother's gaze. "Nicole knows I love her."

"Really? Every day that you push her further and further away from you, she knows that?"

Jayden looked at him, adamant. "I'm not pushing her away. I'm keeping her safe."

"By hurting her?"

Jayden's eyes darkened. "I'd never hurt her. You know that."

"You don't mean to," Brian said, "but you do it every day you don't trust her. I know the feeling. I know how it feels to be locked out when you make a decision. To not be given a choice to be in your life unless you dictated the terms."

Jayden stared at his brother for a long moment a series of emotions—denial, anger, sadness, regret— crossing his face before he hung his head in shame and defeat. "I was only thinking...I never thought about how much...I didn't mean to hurt you. I locked you out because it was my only way to survive." He turned to him. "I'm sorry."

"Me too. I didn't realize how much you were going through either. Dad always told you to look after us, it was an unfair burden."

Jayden shook his head. "Not a burden. A privilege."

Brian opened his mouth to respond when an attractive woman in her sixties took the seat Randolph had vacated and eyed them with interest. "You're both new. What are you reading?"

Jayden rose to his feet. "I'm not much of a reader, but my brother *loves* books," he said and grinned at his brother's glare.

CHAPTER THIRTY-NINE

Nicole stood outside in her mother's garden as fireflies dotted the darkness and the fragrance of purple cornflowers and zinnias floated through the air. She'd had to get out of the house. Her mother knew how to irritate her. Ernestina didn't see anything wrong with calling an adult mixer a book club or casually providing male companions for her friends.

"Nobody pays for anything, sex is not permitted on the premises," Ernestina assured her.

"You sound like a rulebook."

"Of course we have to have rules. We also strongly encourage condom use. You may not get pregnant but you can get other nasty things..."

"Mom—"

"We've very selective in who we let join. Prentice has been a darling helping me."

"Mom."

"And we don't always invite the men, sometimes we just talk amongst ourselves."

"Mom, you don't—"

Ernestina smiled pleased with herself. "What's the danger?"

That's what infuriated her the most. Her mother never saw the danger. What was the danger of having different men exposed to her two young daughters? What was the danger in promising a man one thing then changing your mind?

But the most frustrating part was that she had to accept her. As much as she angered her, she still loved Ernestina. And Nicole knew Ernestina loved her in her own way. That's why Stephanie always stood up for her. She wasn't the best of mothers, but she was theirs. They could have worse.

Nicole heard footsteps in the grass and started to turn but stopped when a deep voice said, "Don't turn around."

Her heart began to race. Jayden. She thought he'd continue to ignore her. "Why not?"

"Because I want to talk to you like this."

She swallowed, trying to keep her body from shaking. "Okay."

"Thanks for helping us out." She heard the footsteps get closer. "Mum's man isn't as bad as I'd feared."

"That's a relief," she said, sensing he was directly behind her. It was a safe topic, but not the one she wanted to hear. "But Jayden—" she began then stopped when she felt large arms wrap around her. For a moment she was transported in time to when she was at her mother's wedding reception surrounded by the scent of azaleas and had first spotted him. When their eyes had met her heart had been his. It was no different now. "Forgive me," he said.

She steeled herself from sinking into his arms; resting her body against his warm chest. "You left me."

"I know."

"You didn't even leave a note or a text or a—"

"I know." He pressed his lips against her cheek, sending a warm shiver through her, then whispered, "Forgive me."

"It hurt."

He pressed a tender kiss on her neck, his voice filled with pain. "I'm sorry."

Nicole blinked back tears. "Don't leave me like that again."

"I won't. Ever."

She took a deep breath and settled into his arms, no longer able to deny how much she wanted to. How wonderful it felt to be close to him again. "Then I forgive you. Can I turn around now?"

She felt him shake his head. "Not yet." He paused. "How's Coco?"

"She's barely eaten anything."

"That doesn't sound good. Think I should come over tonight and check on her?"

"Yes. I think that's a good idea. Can I turn around now?"

"No."

"Why not?"

"I might lose my courage."

"To do what?"

Jayden released his hold and let his arms fall to his side. "If I ask the woman I love to marry me, even though I lied to her, I have a criminal past and I hurt her, what do you think she'd say?"

Nicole spun around. She'd expected a lot of things, but never that. She'd always been a little frightened of the thought of marriage, but as she met Jayden's uncertain gaze she knew he was the man she wanted to walk through life with. Joy flowed through her and warmed her heart. "I know exactly what she'd say, Brown Bear." She cupped his face in her hands and kissed him. "She'd say 'yes.'"

CHAPTER FORTY

A YEAR LATER

"Of all the men in the world, you choose to marry an ex-convict," Aunt Cleo said with disdain as she looked at Nicole's new husband talking to his best man. "You're as ridiculous as your mother." They'd gotten married in a simple ceremony and now hosted the reception in the same hotel courtyard where she and Jayden had met.

"A man was abusing his mother," Nicole said, keeping up the lie the Cassells had asked her to do for Dionne's sake. "He served his time."

"Well at least he didn't say it was self-defense. That would have been uncreative."

"I believe him."

"Of course you do. I'm sure with a face and body like that he got plenty of conjugal visits. Where did you meet him again?"

"I told you. At Mom's wedding last spring." Nicole looked at crowd and spotted Ernestina playfully feeding

Prentice some cake then her gaze shifted to Dionne who was laughing at something Randolph had said. So far the two women looked very happy with their chosen partners.

Aunt Cleo furrowed her brows. "I don't know why I don't remember seeing him."

"He was the one who took me to the hospital."

Her aunt peered closer at him then shook her head. "I still can't place him. But if you say—"

Nicole stopped her words with a hug.

Aunt Cleo stiffened, stunned by the unexpected embrace.

"Thank you Aunty," Nicole said with feeling. "Thank you for believing me all those years ago. Thank you for looking out for me ever since. I'm sorry it's taken me a long time to say that."

Aunt Cleo briefly squeezed her then stepped back. "Well, enough of that silliness. We're not Americans."

Nicole grinned, pleased to see her aunt flustered. "I am."

"I try my best to forget that most times." She gestured to Jayden. "Now go. He looks like he wants to say something to you."

Nicole left her aunt and walked up to Jayden. "You're staring at me."

His gaze slid down her silk and lace wedding dress. "I can't help myself. You look beautiful."

She pretended to straighten his lapel. "And you look dashing."

"Thanks to you." He snapped his fingers as if remembering something. "That's right. I wanted to ask you something."

"What?"

A smile danced on his lips. "A few guests want to know if you are going to toss the bouquet."

"By 'guests' you mean my mother, don't you?" Nicole looked at her mother who was wiggling her fingers at her with a hopeful smile. "You can tell her absolutely not."

Jayden laughed and drew her close. "I thought you'd say that."

She gazed up at him. "I can't wait to go home."

"Home," Jayden said, caressing the word as if it was something sacred. He kissed her then whispered, "With you I already am."

ABOUT THE AUTHOR

Dara Girard, an award-winning, national bestselling author of more than forty novels, from romance to suspense, loves telling stories.

Born in the US to immigrant parents, Dara enjoys pulling from her Jamaican, British, Nigerian heritage and exposure to various cultures to bring what reviewers and fans call "vivid emotional stories" to life. She is best known for her popular Henson Series, the mysterious Clifton Sisters, and the fun Black Stockings Society.

You can write her at:
contactdara@daragirard.com
or
P.O. Box 10345
Silver Spring, MD 20914
If you'd like to receive a reply, please send a self-addressed stamped envelope.

Visit her website to sign up for her newsletter and get sneak peeks, monthly updates on new releases, and special offers.

For more information visit
www.daragirard.com